BLACK RIVER

BLACK RIVER

LEE MARTIN

VACA MOUNTAIN PRESS
VACAVILLE, CALIFORNIA, USA

Vaca Mountain Press
Paperback ISBN 13: 978-1-952380-32-7
Kindle ISBN 13: 978-1-952380-33-4

Also available in
Large Print ISBN 13: 978-1-952380-34-1

Library of Congress Catalog Card Number: 93-90263

Interior design by Eddie Vincent, ENC Graphic Services
Cover design by Deirdre Wait for ENC Graphic Services
Cover images © Getty Images

Published by Vaca Mountain Press

Visit Lee Martin Westerns on Facebook.

To all of my wonderful family,
and in the fond memory of
my beloved mother,
my beautiful sister Arlene,
our rough riding brothers,
and for Jim Liontas.

BLACK RIVER

ONE

*S*he stood alone on the rise in the windswept grass, long black hair moving in the wind as she shaded her eyes from the rising sun. Her ragged dress whipped about her with her right leg bared below the knee, her right arm exposed and caked with blood. A rope was tied and knotted at her left ankle.

Nathan Reed lay deep in the tall grass some twenty feet up from the Rio Grande. His buckskins were hot in the sun, and he pushed his wide-brimmed hat up from his sweaty, lined brow. Oakley, a young private in torn and bloody uniform, was there with him. A half mile back, they had stumbled over a dozen wagons and a lot of dead men.

"Nathan," Oakley murmured, sweat on his round, pink face. "I don't know how she got away, but we got to get her. The Mescalero might come back."

"It's a trap," Nathan whispered.

"You mean they staked her out?"

"Looks like it."

"What are we gonna do? If it's a trap, they know we're here. Don't they ever give up?"

1

Nathan gazed across the wide rolling sea of grass in all directions. Most of it tall and gangly and touched with various colors, some of the flowers remaining. The only trees were cottonwoods back down at the river. There were clumps of brush and scattered sage with its pungent smell. It was a hot afternoon with rising wind in the fall of 1879, and New Mexico Territory had never been more hostile.

In his early thirties, tall with a body hard and muscled from a life on the frontier, wearing a fringed buckskin shirt and a low-slung Colt, Nathan was a man with burning anger and a thirst for vengeance that had nothing to do with the Apache. He had to get to Black River alive. He had to kill a man, or the pain in his gut would never ease.

Crossing the land, he had found Oakley, who was nursing a wounded shoulder, the only survivor of his patrol and being tracked by Mescaleros. The two had barely escaped with their lives. And now they were in trouble again.

"Can't be many of them," Nathan whispered. "They'd be on us by now."

"So what are we gonna do?"

"Cover me."

Leaving his hat and canteen, Nathan moved forward on his belly. His revolver in his big right hand, his hunting knife in his left, he began to inch through the tall grass as it weaved to betray him. A bug crawled over his arm.

As he slid up the slope toward the woman, Nathan blew the sweat from his mouth as it ran down his weathered face from around his strong nose and down his carved cheekbones. His pale blue eyes narrowed to slits, and his hard jaw was set with grim determination. A day's growth of beard darkened his skin. His sandy hair was damp and long to his shoulders.

He paused to peer through the grass. He saw the stake near her as well as something farther away to her right, something trying very hard to hide.

Nathan moved within ten feet of her. He could see her young face with delicate features, fair skin caked with dirt, numb horror holding her silent.

"Get down," he whispered.

Slowly, she turned her head and gazed toward him, barely seeing him. She stiffened, but she was coming to life, her hand at her throat as if to stifle a scream. Her dark eyes were wild and round, yet she was too terrified to move.

Nathan slid closer, knowing any moment one of the Apaches would be upon him. His heart was pounding so loud he feared they would hear. Sweat covered his back and chest, down around his belly. He could barely breathe as he knew he had to move.

He leaped to his feet, rushing her with knife in hand.

As he reached her and dropped down to slash at the ankle rope, he heard her gasp. He shoved her down and spun about, then saw the two Apaches, and his gut wrenched.

They were charging him, their square, hard faces streaked with paint, eyes blazing, lips curved down, short black hair bound back with headbands of soiled white cloth, bodies bare but for breechcloths and leggings, huge chests and muscles gleaming. Each had a big knife and were coming fast.

Oakley fired, and one of them spun around and fell on his back in the grass. The other kept coming. Oakley's second shot missed the warrior. Terror ran through Nathan.

Nathan raised his six-gun and fired, hitting the charging

man in the chest, but the warrior didn't stop and slammed into Nathan, knocking him backward with knife slashing past his neck.

They clinched, and Nathan's knife went flying as he tried to hold onto his six-gun. His free hand on the Apache's face, Nathan thrust him aside, but the Apache was back upon him with rising fury. Nathan fired right into the man's middle, but the warrior didn't stop and kept slashing at him, then charged and grappled as Nathan's six-gun was jerked from his hand.

The Apache was so powerful that Nathan's life was about to be slashed away. He seized the Apache's thick, muscled wrists, fighting to hold back the big knife. They crashed backwards, the Apache falling on top of him.

The knife was being brought down, slowly, despite Nathan's struggle. And suddenly, with renewed strength, Nathan jerked the man's hand and sent the knife down and up, into the big chest, dead center.

The startled warrior's mouth opened. He stared down at Nathan as death tore the color from his face. And then he fell on Nathan, nearly crushing him. Frantic, Nathan rolled the warrior away, and he sat up, wiping blood from his buckskin shirt, his breath in short gasps.

As Nathan tried to get to his feet, he was conscious of movement behind him, realizing the first Apache was not dead and he was between the warrior and Oakley's rifle. He could almost feel the knife sliding into his back even as he spun, knowing he was too late to stop it.

But in the same split second, the woman had jerked the stake from the ground and shoved it into the Apache's back. The wounded warrior's face went crazed with pain, and he turned his knife on her. Nathan seized the Apache by the leg and threw him aside and in the clear.

As the Apache staggered sideways, Oakley fired, and this time, the warrior was downed for good.

Breathing hard, Nathan checked both dead men to be sure. Even in death, the Apache were frightening. No better warrior lived on the frontier, and no other sent such terror through the hearts of men.

Still kneeling as he holstered his Colt, Nathan looked up at the young woman. She was in her mid-twenties with dirty face and grass in her long raven hair. There were bruises on her bare arm already turning blue, but the blood was not hers. She wavered, barely able to stand.

The bloody two-foot stake was still in her hand.

Realizing the fight was over, she let the stake fall from her fingers. Her eyes were dark blue and round and dazed with shock. She tried to draw her dress to cover her bare leg.

Slowly, she let herself drop to the grass on her knees.

Abruptly, she became hysterical, sobbing and weeping, burying her face in her hands, shaking her head as if it would all go away.

Oakley hurried to Nathan's side. "It was just the two of them. But more could show up anytime. We gotta go, Nathan."

Nathan was fighting for breath and feeling cold all over. He retrieved his knife and sheathed it at his belt.

The woman was still sobbing, but she looked up through her quivering hands as she slowly lowered them. She had a good face with high cheekbones, her tangled, raven hair spread all over her shoulders and curling around her throat like a shawl.

Oakley bent near her. "Who are you, Ma'am?"

She choked on her tears. "Leslie Cromwell."

"You kin to Jason Cromwell?" Oakley asked, startled.

"Yes. I was married to his younger brother." Her voice was wavering and forced. "I was widowed, and Jason sent for me. There were twenty of us and some wagons, coming up from Mesilla. They're all dead."

"We saw 'em, ma'am," Oakley said as he handed Nathan his hat. "But we can't help 'em now. We gotta keep movin'."

Nathan struggled to his feet and reached down to lift her up in his arms, cradling her like a child as she wept and clung to his buckskin fringe, her face buried at his chest.

They went back down to the river, keeping along the sandy, lazy water as the banks shielded them from view. Walking north, they prayed silently the other Apaches had not returned to find their two missing brothers.

When they reached a deep cut in the river banks, they rested. Leslie had stopped crying and sat hugging herself, still wrapped in the horror she had seen. Oakley knelt by her, offering her jerky, and she took it but couldn't eat. He spoke quietly.

"We was on patrol out of Fort Royale, up by Black River, and we was crossin' the prairie. Them Apaches had buried themselves in the dirt and just come right up outta the ground. I was the only one got away, but they was on my trail. If Nathan Reed hadn't come along afore dark, I'd be dead. They got our horses, all right, but me and Nathan, we got clean away in the night."

Oakley helped her to stand. She was walking slowly as Nathan led the way, Winchester balanced in his left hand, his right hand near his holster.

They kept walking north along the shallow river, keeping

down below the bank and only stopping for Nathan to care for Oakley's wound, which was bleeding again. Then Nathan scouted along the water's edge, sometimes slipping up the dirt wall to peer across the rolling land.

If more Apaches came, their trail would be easy to find. Time was their only hope. And those clouds on the northern horizon. As the sun rose high in the sky, Nathan became weary, but he knew the others were in worse shape. The girl could hardly walk.

He made false trails wherever he could, and he cut a clump of brush to cover their tracks.

Night fell, and they crossed the shallow river to the Arizona side, making a cold camp against the high bank where they could hopefully see anyone coming. Clouds moved across the starry sky.

Leslie knelt by the icy water to wash her face and hands as the chill of darkness cut like ice. When she returned, her dark eyes reflected the shine of the rising moon.

They ate jerky and drank cold water from the river, refilling their canteens and listening to the night sounds.

Oakley shook his head. "All this for fifteen dollars a month. Saddle sores. Shoveling out the stable. Livin' on hardtack, bacon and beans. I must be loco."

Later, as the woman slept curled up against the dirt bank, Oakley turned to Nathan, speaking softly.

"Jason Cromwell, he and his brother moved in about three years ago. Bought a couple stores and a tradin' company, deliverin' goods to the army and the reservation. Any contract for horses and beef and corn or whatever, Cromwell's tradin' company wins the bid. That Indian agent and our Captain Paine, I figure they got some kind of deal with Cromwell."

7

Nathan sipped his coffee, listening with interest.

"What's worse," Oakley added, "the other traders and ranchers at Black River, they're hoppin' mad. They been accusin' Cromwell of workin' with rustlers to get cheap cattle so he can undercut their prices."

"This Cromwell, is he getting rich?"

Oakley shook his head. "They're usin' vouchers right and left. They're either hoardin' their money or spendin' more than they make. And there's some talk they was feedin' five hundred more Mescalero than even exists on the reservation, and chargin' the government for it."

"What's the army done about it?"

"There was two investigators from the Department of Justice, and one from the Indian Inspector's. One got killed when he was bucked off in some canyon, and the others left without findin' no proof anything was wrong. Cromwell even convinced 'em the extra Apaches he was billin' for had taken off. Paine backed him up. Now I think them phantom Apaches are back again."

"Who's the commanding officer?"

"We had us a Major, and he was a good man, but he got shot in some alley in Black River. No one ever does anything about the killin's."

"Sounds like a nice place."

"Yeah, even worse than Lincoln. Over there they got men like Trabajo, fast guns that kill for hire. Over here, they don't bother with all that nicety. They just shoot you down cold."

Nathan leaned back in the pale light. He was absorbing the information, and it was giving him a picture of Black River he didn't find too friendly. But if the man he was after was in Black River, nothing could stop him.

He took the first watch while Oakley slept.

Nathan had a chance to study Leslie, even as clouds continued to cut the moonlight. She appeared to have nice, gentle features. Her form was went rounded, and her long black hair had to look grand when clean and shining. But she had something else, a toughness shielding vulnerability, reminding him of his late wife, which brought painful memory.

He lay back and stared up at the stars. He could see General Crook's stony gaze, the graying mustache and beard, could hear the aging man's deep voice, echoing in the mountains of Arizona Territory.

"Nathan," he had said, "I need you here. But if that Wolf fellow has surfaced over at Black River, then I know you got to go. But you watch yourself. Any man who carves his initial on the bodies of his victims, he's a cold-blooded killer who'll give no quarter. You're going to need help."

"I sent for Quincy," Nathan had said.

Crook had grinned. "That scalawag?"

Nathan thought fondly of the general as he stared at the sky, but life had been bitter these last three years. When he had learned from an army news dispatch that a dead man with a W carved on him had been found near Black River a few months ago, he had written Quincy to meet him.

The raid on his ranch had left one ranch hand dead in the field with Wolf's mark on him. The other hands and his family had died in the fire. Nathan would never rest until Wolf was hanged.

He turned as he heard Leslie moan.

Suddenly, her eyes were open, and she was staring at Nathan. She sat up slowly. Frantic, she looked around. When she saw the sleeping soldiers, she drew a deep breath, then shivered in the cold and hugged herself for warmth.

"I'm afraid," she whispered.

Nathan slid closer and sat near her. "Could be we' re in the clear."

She moved a little closer to him, seeking comfort in his strength. Her voice was breaking with emotion.

"When they hit the Cromwell wagons, I was hiding in the brush by the creek where I had been washing. It was a horrible sight. When the Apaches left, I came out of the brush to see if anyone was alive. Two of them came back and found me. But before they could do anything, they suddenly stopped, and one put his ear to the ground. They must have known you were coming because they dragged me away from the wagons."

Nathan didn't answer. He was hurting for her, and she continued, her words fading to a whisper.

"They made me walk to this high place, then staked me out like a goat. I kept falling down, but they poked me with a spear and made me stand. I guess they were going to kill me."

"They don't have time for prisoners."

"I prayed and prayed, and you came."

Nathan swallowed hard. His wife and son must have prayed, trapped inside the burning house with two of his men, while fierce Comancheros had swarmed over the ranch. Nathan hadn't been there to fight for them, but he had saved Leslie, and he felt better for it.

He glanced at her. "How long ago did you lose your husband?"

"Six months ago. We were coming out of the church on our wedding day in Mesilla. Paul was so happy, and they were throwing rice at us. Then there was a shot, and he was dead, right there on the steps. They never learned who did it."

"You ever meet his brother, this Jason?"

"A year ago. He was in Mesilla with one of his freight caravans when Paul and I were engaged. And there was another brother, Titus, a terrible man with no manners, looking me up and down like an animal, but he was only there a few days before the wedding, and I never saw him again."

"So now Jason's sent for you."

"I have no other family," she said softly. "My parents died of the fever in St. Louis. I mostly lived with an aunt in Texas until she died. That's where I met Paul Cromwell. But what about you, Nathan?"

He hesitated, words choking up in him. He had not told his story to anyone but General Crook, keeping the pain and anger locked inside. Yet her dark blue eyes were wide and glistening in the starlight. Her delicate lips were parted. There was a softness about her, compassion so ready in her gaze.

"Lost my wife and eight-year-old son. Three years ago. Comancheros. White men riding with Comanches. Led by a man called Wolf. Down in Texas."

"I'm so sorry."

Nathan's voice was breaking. The agony of not having been there to fight for his family was still a hard rock in his gut. Even now he felt tears brimming in his eyes.

"I was up north when it happened and had no way of knowin'. It was a year before I got the letter from an old trapper friend, Quincy, tellin' me how the house was burned down and everyone in it. I near went crazy. But Quincy wrote how he hunted Wolf and his Comancheros with the army, but the devils had just vanished. Seems after my ranch, the raids had stopped."

"So you didn't go back?"

"The trail was a year old. And no one ever saw Wolf's face and lived to tell about it. I figured if anyone could have found 'em, it would have been Quincy. And I was scoutin' for General Crook in the Black Hills on a rough campaign. I couldn't leave then, and after that, I didn't want to go home. Quincy took care of everything. Even sold the place for me."

"He sounds like a good friend."

"He'll be waitin' for me at Black River."

"I'm so sorry, Nathan."

"I'd been a scout when I met her. I tried to keep the ranch goin', but the army kept calling me back. I left my wife and son because Crook needed me, sent for me. While Custer was being overrun by the Sioux, my family was being murdered. There I was up there in the Black Hills, fighting to keep Crook's men from starving, and I wasn't doin' nothin' for my own."

"You couldn't help it, Nathan."

"Yeah, I could have," he muttered, realizing for the first time that his grief was tied to more guilt than he had accepted. "I never should have married in the first place. I was a wanderin' man. I couldn't stay put. There was always a new trail somewhere. Scoutin' was an excuse, that's all."

"But you loved her."

"God, how I loved her."

"She understood you, Nathan, but she married you just the same. Did she ever ask you to stay put, to never leave?"

"No."

"Then she loved you, Nathan."

Tears ran down his weathered face. He was hurting so bad, his insides were churning, even as he wiped his eyes with the back of his hand. Nathan's agony would never end until Wolf was finished, one way or another.

To her surprise and his, he reached out and drew her against him, cradling her in his arms. She willingly settled against his chest, knees drawn up over his thighs. After a time, she stopped quivering, and she slept, sometimes moaning in her nightmares.

Nathan felt such sadness, he could hardly breathe.

He was holding a woman he barely knew, trying to keep her warm, her slim fingers wound into the fringe on his shirt. Memories of his wife were all the more painful now that he had allowed himself to speak of it. Yet he felt stronger for bringing out the words.

He held Leslie for hours, fighting to stay awake, and all the while thinking of his wife. Then Oakley took a turn at watch, and Nathan fell asleep with Leslie snug in his arms, giving him comfort and the first deep rest he had known for a long time. He slept so soundly, he didn't feel the soft drizzle of rain.

When he awakened at first light, Leslie's black hair was covering most of her face and she had nestled more comfortably in his embrace, her fingers still wrapped in the fringe for security. Nathan held her a little tighter, realizing they were all damp and the clouds were threatening.

Suddenly, Oakley was kneeling, his voice in a whisper. "I hear somethin'."

TWO

*O*akley's warning sent an icy chill running through Nathan, who shook Leslie gently and put his hand on her mouth. Eyes wide, terror colored her face, and he removed his hand. She began to shake with fear as he set her carefully aside.

The western river bank rose some ten feet above them. The silvery Rio Grande spread before then in first light, and to the east above the other bank, the trail to Fort Roy ale and safety was waiting.

Nathan signaled them to stay low, and he slid up the wet bank to where the grass was thin. He removed his hat and pulled himself up enough to see through the blades.

What he saw sent a wave of terror through him. A dozen Mescalero were riding south along the river, just fifty feet away from them. He slid back down and gathered the others, moving slowly and silently north along the bank, praying the warriors did not tum to the river and find their tracks.

It was starting to rain, and he whispered a prayer of thanks. Oakley was leading the woman. Now it was pouring rain, and there was no time to look back. They ran, leaving footprints in the sand, even as rain beat on them. The river was rising fast, but they dared not venture across as yet.

They ran until the woman collapsed. Nathan lifted her in his arms, then threw her over his left shoulder, his left arm around her legs. She lay quiet, and he kept running. They were slipping and sliding in the rain, and the river was still rising. They had to take a chance and cross before it was too late.

With furtive glances downriver, they splashed into the icy water. It was waist high and the current was strong and swift. Nathan swung Leslie around and into his arms. She clung to him, her face at his neck. They reached the other side, and he set her down, taking her hand.

Staying between the river and the east bank, they moved north, praying the Apache had taken shelter from the storm.

The water was rising fast, and soon they had to climb out onto the bank for safety, but it was so dark and the rain so heavy, they themselves could not see more than a few hundred feet.

"The fort's that way," Oakley said, pointing northwest. "But we'll pass a couple ranches afore we get there. If anyone's alive."

As they walked, Oakley filled them in on Victorio.

"Two months ago, Victorio was on the reservation. He was accused of murder more than once. And one day, he scared that Indian agent so bad, the man went for the soldiers. When Victorio heard the bugle, he knew they was coming, so he and his men took off. They killed a couple sheepmen on the way south.

"He went to Mexico but came back. He killed some soldiers at Ojo Caliente and took over forty horses. We went after him, and he killed some of us and stole as many horses again.

"We couldn't stop 'im. And then a group of nearly one

hundred and fifty men from the range country went after 'im. He killed a bunch of them and got away. Some men from Mesilla tried to get him, but they were ambushed and a lot of 'em killed. Then Victorio attacked two army supply trains and got away again. Now we figure all these stray Apaches are lookin' to join up with him."

They moved across the open, rolling land. They were soaked through. Only Nathan in his buckskin shirt had some protection. The woman's hand felt void of warmth, limp in his grasp. She was all the more pale, and he was worried.

But as night fell again, they saw a ranch house along a raging creek. Smoke rose from the chimney only to be beaten down by the rain. Horses huddled in the corrals, so it appeared safe.

They stumbled up to the door, and Nathan pounded. A wooden shutter slid aside from a window, and a lamp was lifted to throw a glow on them. Soon, the door was unbarred and opened, and a bearded old Mexican brought them inside.

"Apache?" the rancher asked.

The men nodded while the sight of the blazing hearth made Leslie gasp, and she hurried to kneel before it. She was so wet and colorless, the old man threw a blanket around her. There was another room, and he told her to get some dry clothes in there. She hurried into the sanctuary, closing the door behind her.

Oakley and Nathan knelt by the fire as the old man brought them coffee. He had a thin little nose and protruding belly in a scrawny body. His thick beard had streaks of gray, and his dark eyes were friendly.

"I'm Nathan Reed. This here's Oakley, and the lady is Leslie Cromwell."

The old man was surprised by her name but nodded. "I'm Chavez. Jose Chavez. This is my ranch. Were they Mescaleros?"

"Sure were," Oakley said. "They got the patrol I was with. Nathan here, he saved my hide. Then we come on some wagons where everyone was dead but the lady. We saw some more Apaches down by the river, but they was headed south."

"I have seen nothing," Chavez said, his face twisted. "But that might explain why my two hands did not come back last night."

Leslie came out wearing a man's shirt and trousers. She had blankets around her and hurried to the fireside where she spread her tattered dress on a chair to dry as if desperately clinging to her femininity. The men stood up and away, making room. She sat down, warming her hands.

Chavez brought her coffee. She placed her hands around the cup, feeling its warmth. While Chavez fussed over some cans and pots, she looked up at Nathan and managed a weak smile.

Soon a pot of beans was dangling over the fire, and before long, they were sitting at the rough table on handmade chairs, devouring their food.

"Maybe I will go to the fort with you," Chavez said carefully. "Then I will go to Black River for supplies."

"Are you alone here?" she asked.

"Oh, no, I have two hands, but they are out with the sheep. I have got to buy more food. They eat like there was ten of them."

Leslie gazed at him, uncertain, but she finally accepted the story. She was so weary, she went into the backroom to sleep in Chavez's bed, the door closed behind her. Nathan was still worried about her but rested with the men around the hearth as he explained about Leslie.

"She is a nice Señora," Chavez said, "but this Jason Cromwell and his brother, they are bad men."

"I hear things have been rough around here," Nathan said.

Oakley yawned. "Some of the cattlemen, they just go out and shoot the sheep like they was rabbits."

"We know Jason Cromwell is behind some of it," Chavez said, "but we cannot prove it. He is a man who loans money to my people, then takes their notes and mortgages so he can foreclose and rent out their land. He has a lot of men who ride for him. And he deals with rustlers to get enough cattle to sell to the army."

"Have you lost sheep?" Nathan asked.

"My land is poor, so he has not come for me yet. But I think the Apache have come first. I worry, Señors, that I will never see my hands anymore."

"You'd better come with us," Oakley said.

"I will come, but not because I am afraid. I will come to help protect the Señora. And I need supplies."

"You can get them at the fort," Oakley suggested.

"No, Señor Oakley. At the fort, there is only Cromwell's trading company. I want to go to Black River and buy from those he is trying to destroy."

Before dawn, after a quick breakfast, they saddled and mounted Chavez's horses, heading northwest in the drizzling rain. The rancher had supplied slickers for Leslie, still in a man's clothes, and Oakley. He and Nathan wore heavy leather jackets with wool collars. A floppy hat was given to Leslie to wear.

Rain poured off the brims of their hats. It was nearly nightfall when Oakley jubilantly recognized a grove of cottonwood along a creekbed.

"Ain't far now," he said.

The fort had high walls with a blockhouse by the main gate and another in the opposite comer. The buildings were in rows around the open parade ground. Outside the walls were many tents, corrals and outbuildings.

Inside the walls, one of the buildings had Cromwell's sign on it as post trader. "They sort of appointed themselves," Oakley muttered.

Lanterns hung on posts, and they were led to the captain's quarters facing the parade area. His ornate office was in front of his private rooms. Fine paintings of the west hung on the walls. Relics of the War between the States were posted, including a shining saber. Furniture was plush, and his desk had a shining walnut top.

Paine was a stocky man with a square face and chilling blue eyes. He sat behind his desk as they stood before him. He didn't change his stone expression as be heard Oakley's story, until he learned Leslie was not only widowed but had an important name.

"Cromwell?" he repeated, his face brightening.

The captain stood up and hurriedly helped her to a chair. "You take my quarters. I'll bunk with one of my officers. The Lieutenant's wife will bring you clothes. And tomorrow, I'll get word to Jason."

"Sir," Oakley said, standing erect, "Mr. Reed lost his horse helping us."

Paine frowned. "I'll see what I can do, Mr. Reed, but I don't promise. Now seems to me your name is kind of familiar. Did you scout for General Crook? Up in the Black Hills?"

"Yes, sir, in '76."

"Were they really eating their horses? Why did Crook take a chance on that march with hardly any provisions?"

Nathan was annoyed with the questions and didn't answer. But he knew the truth. Crook had taken a calculated risk against Nathan's advice. Abandoned, broken horses had been eaten while a reporter had sat writing out his story. A disaster of a trip. Yet Nathan had nothing but respect for Crook and refused to comment.

"So why are you here?" Paine asked. "Did General Crook send you?"

Nathan shook his head and fell silent.

Annoyed, Paine became impatient. "Did the army send you?"

Again, Nathan shook his head, his pale blue eyes gleaming like ice.

Paine studied him but finally gave up and sat on the edge of his desk. "I would mount a campaign to run down those red devils, but I would be chasing ghosts. And this fort is the only protection for Black River. I can't spare enough men."

"Oakley deserves a citation," Nathan said.

Paine shook his head. "He's been busted twice. I see no reason to reward him for doing his job as a soldier. But right now, he has leave to see the surgeon."

Nathan frowned. "I think the surgeon should also have a look at Mrs. Cromwell."

"Yes, yes, of course," Paine said, embarrassed.

Everyone left her to rest, except Nathan, who stepped back inside. He walked over to look down at her and put his hand on her forehead. She was burning bot.

"You'll be all right," he said. "But you need to break that fever."

He started to turn away, and she caught his hand. He gazed down at her dark, gleaming eyes and flickering smile.

"You saved my life," she whispered.

"And you saved mine."

Her smile settled, and then she sobered. "Mr. Reed, I may need a friend in Black River."

"You got three of us. And Quincy will be there."

"But they can't help me. You can."

Nathan paused, her hand small and cold in his. He wasn't sure what she wanted, but he could only nod his head. He knew he would do anything for her.

She smiled once more, and her hand fell away.

Nathan gazed at her a long moment. Her raven hair was in contrast with her dark-blue eyes, and her fair skin had been burned by the sun, but she was a gorgeous woman. Were he not devastated with guilt from the loss of his wife, were he free of pain, he would be trying to reserve her for himself. As it was, he was no good to anyone with memory burning a hole in his gut.

Nathan tipped his hat and left her. He walked to the stable where Chavez was waiting and already making his bed in the straw. A lantern burned low near the entrance. The place smelled of manure and sweat and horses and leather.

"That nice Señora will marry Jason Cromwell?"

"I don't know."

"It would be a terrible thing."

They made their beds in the straw with blankets supplied by the army, and they were weary. They finally slept as rain pounded the roof, but during the night, Nathan felt a sudden chill, and he opened his eyes in time to see the knife coming down at his chest.

21

THREE

*N*athan rolled aside in the straw as the blade cut his left arm.

He seized the big wrists and stared into the wild face of a young but ugly, bearded man. He thrust him away and got to his knees, still holding onto the man's wrists and struggling to keep the knife from cutting him more. They grunted and strained, and the attacker tried to kick him.

They pounded each other in the clinch, sweat covering them as they groaned and struggled, then broke apart.

Nathan leaped to his feet, freeing the man and jumping back. With a snarl, the ugly man charged with the knife, slashing past Nathan's neck as Nathan struck him on the head with his fist.

Furious and momentarily stunned, the assailant rolled over and sprang up with his revolver aimed at Nathan. Before the man could pull the trigger, Nathan's Colt was in his hand, firing point blank. His bullet hit the man square in the chest, and the attacker gasped, mouth rounded, doubling up and dropping to his knees, staring at Nathan.

As the dead man rolled over in the straw, Chavez got to his feet, rubbing sleep from his eyes and staring at the scene. Then he helped Nathan remove his jacket.

"Señor, you make a lot of noise."

"Sorry about that."

Chavez rolled up Nathan's shirtsleeve from his arm, then washed the blood away with his bandanna and water from a nearby hanging bucket. The knife had just seared the flesh, and it would heal.

But Nathan was perplexed about the attack. Even if Wolf was in the area, he'd have no reason to know that Nathan was after him, nor would he have any worry about Nathan being a danger to him. No, the killer had been sent by someone unknown to Nathan.

Two soldiers came running, one a burly sergeant. "What's going on here?" the sergeant growled, his red mustache twitching as he stared at the heap in the straw. "Who is that dead man?"

Chavez wrapped Nathan's arm with Nathan's bandanna. "I know him, Señor Sergeant. It was young Beeler. His father sells cattle to Señor Cromwell."

But later that morning in Captain Paine's office, a thin man representing Cromwell denied everything. His name was Rachet. He had a thin face and a thin black mustache. His thin black hair was pasted down. A good wind could blow him away. But he had steel-gray eyes and looked plenty dangerous.

"We stopped dealing with Beeler some time ago," Rachet said with an icy voice. "We found some of the cattle the Beelers was selling us were stolen."

Paine leaned back in his wooden chair behind his big desk

and put his fingertips together. In the room were Chavez, Nathan, the sergeant with the red mustache, and Rachet. There was no sign of Leslie.

But Paine had trimmed his hair and was cleanly shaven. His blue uniform had been sponged and pressed, and he looked like a man who had courting on his mind. He seemed not to care one bit about Nathan's wound nor the dead man in the barn.

Chavez tugged at his beard. "Señor Captain, Beeler bad his pistol pointed at Señor Reed. Before he could pull the trigger, Señor Reed drew his gun and killed him. I have never seen a man draw so fast. And it was a fair fight."

"Yes, yes," Paine said, impatient. "Sergeant, do something with the body. Mr. Rachet, you can go back to your store. I will be driving Mrs. Cromwell into Black River. Mr. Reed, you and Mr. Chavez may leave anytime you wish."

But Chavez's description of Nathan's speed with a gun had caught Rachet's attention, and he looked Nathan over with a cold glance.

"Then why have I never heard of you, Mr. Reed?"

Nathan merely looked at him with no response.

"Mr. Reed," said Paine, "was Crook's personal scout."

Rachet sneered. "Did he run you off?"

Nathan just looked at him with disdain.

Rachet turned on his heel and left with Chavez and the sergeant, leaving Nathan and the Captain to glare at each other. There was something about Paine that Nathan detested. He had seen it in other men, and when they were officers in the United States Army, it was all the more irritating.

"Yes, Mr. Reed?"

"You know full well that man was paid to kill me."

"By whom?"

"It's your post. You tell me."

It was then that the back door to the office opened, and looking stunning in a blue dress with blue velvet jacket, Leslie came into view. Her long black hair was shining and soft on her shoulders. Her face was clean and peach colored, her dark eyes sparkling. She was beautiful.

Nathan stared at her, trying to reconcile this image with that of the terrified prisoner in a tattered dress.

Paine gazed at her with admiration and glee. He bowed slightly before her, then turned to glare at Nathan.

"Mr. Reed, you may go. Unless you are offering your services as scout."

Nathan frowned. "I have other plans."

"Am I to understand you do not want to scout for us?"

"That's right."

"You're not as brave as I thought."

Nathan looked at him a long solemn moment, his blue eyes so cold and icy, the officer drew himself up in defense. Then Nathan turned to look at the lovely woman who was lifting her hand toward him. He moved over to her, her fingers sliding into his.

"Thank you, Nathan. Private Oakley and I, we'd be dead if it wasn't for you."

She stood on her tiptoes, her slim hand on his arm, and kissed his weathered cheek. It sent a wave of startled emotion charging through him, leaving him shaken as she drew back. He felt another tremor run through him, all the way down to his boots.

Nathan swallowed hard. Her slim fingers slid from his grasp, and he walked to the door, then turned to have another look at her. Being around her made him feel right fine.

Paine moved in front of her. "Good day, Mr. Reed."

Outside in the drizzling rain, Nathan wiped his hot brow with the back of his hand. Chavez was waiting with his four horses by the stable. Oakley was there in clean uniform and slicker, grinning as he shook Nathan's hand.

"You ever need me, Nathan, you holler."

Chavez planned to use two of his horses to pack supplies. He was mounted on a sorrel, and Nathan was given the black horse.

"That horse sure is homely," Oakley commented of the black. "His legs are short and heavy."

"He's a mountain horse," Chavez said.

Nathan reined the black around. It had a soft mouth.

He leaned on the pommel to gaze at Oakley. "Watch yourself. The Captain don't like me much, and he's going to associate us."

"I ain't worried. And thanks again."

When Chavez and Nathan rode out of the fort, both huddled in their leather jackets, Nathan turned in the saddle to look back at the waving Oakley who stood in the open gate. The sight was choking him up, and he turned to glance at Chavez, who was busy leading his two extra horses.

Rain was heavier now, and they pulled their hats down tight, following the canyon road toward Black River.

This was cow country with plenty of grass sweeping the rolling hills. There were some scattered junipers and more cottonwoods along the big creek. It was called Black River for some of the black lava that was bare along the bank for about a mile. He glanced towards the distant mountains to their far right, blue against the sky with some streaks of snow.

Nathan liked what he saw, but he couldn't enjoy it. He was on a mission, and the fury within him was a driving force. He wasn't ready to tell anyone why he was here. He didn't know whom he could trust. Wolf could be at Black River because he had friends. The Comanchero could be rebuilding his army after being silent for three years.

Chavez spoke with annoyance. "Captain Paine is so afraid of Victoria coming back, he keeps most of his soldiers in the fort. And the Mescaleros we saw, I heard from the sergeant they stole horses and then went to some ranch and killed some sheep. Maybe they killed my men."

"So what are you going to do?"

"Get supplies and try to hire more men. And now, Señor, there is the town of Black River where men die so easy. Señor Cromwell and his brother have a large house at the east end of town."

Black River was spread along the main trail in the wide canyon between the high, rolling hills. Up high, there were scattered trees and clumps of brush, but grass was plentiful.

The town had a big long building set forth as the courthouse, but signs showed that parts of it were rented out to merchants. Cromwell's Trading Company was one of them and was situated on the first floor with signs on the windows. The sheriff's office was on the other end.

As they rode into town, the hotel was on the left, followed by stores and houses, while on the right was a school, the courthouse and sheriff's office, a small church, and more stores and some saloons and cafes. Behind these buildings were homes built up the slopes. Everything was on the north side of the big creek except where it crossed the main trail at the west end. A wooden bridge marked the entrance to town.

There were some wagons and mules scattered about. A few old men sat under the roof overhangs. In front of one store, boots and saddles were displayed just out of the wet. Not much was moving in the rain.

Nathan went looking for Quincy, first at the hotel and saloons and then the various supply stores, but there was no sign of the old man. He was worried Quincy might have run into the Mescaleros. He needed Quincy, who knew more about Wolf's mode of operations than anyone.

As he and Chavez were entering the cantina at the east end of town, a small Mexican woman in her fifties, wearing a shawl about her head and shoulders, appeared from a nearby store. She had an aristocratic but nice face and fiery eyes. She looked at Chavez with disdain.

"Señor, you still smell like your sheep."

Chavez bowed. "Señora, you smell like Señor Cromwell's money."

She drew herself up, nose in the air. "At least I am working, Señor."

"This man, he owns you."

"No one owns Lupe."

He looked her over as he moved closer. "Maybe I would like to."

"You need a shave and a bath. Your clothes would stand up by themselves. And you are too skinny."

"If I have a shave and a bath, will you like me?"

She looked him over stiffly, then spun on her heels and walked on up the street, back arched.

"Someday," Chavez said, grinning, "I will have time to make love to that one."

"She didn't seem interested."

"You are wrong, Señor. I see fire in her eyes. The fire is for Jose Chavez."

"Then why don't you take a bath?"

"Someday, Señor. Someday."

They ate at the empty cantina at the east end of town. It was near the slope leading to the big mansion with its wide steps and columns. Nathan asked questions of the sheepman as they lingered over their coffee.

"What about the sheriff?"

"Eichner. He is paid by Cromwell. Everyone knows it. He has two deputies who are not. One was killed a week ago. Shot in the back in an alley like the major. Men die here, Señor. No one does anything. Even the U.S. Marshal does not come here. The judge refuses ID come here to hold court. Governor Wallace has sent for help from Washington. One died. The others left. Nothing has changed."

"And I reckon there's no organized militia."

"No, but Cromwell has his own army of killers. I have heard he has forty or fifty men out in the hills. And he has men like the Corley brothers who laugh when they kill my people. The law looks the other way."

Later, Nathan went to the sheriff's office in the courthouse while Chavez did his business. Nathan had been told the sheriff was on Cromwell's payroll, but he had to make his own judgment. He needed the sheriff to fight Wolf, not Jason

Cromwell or his brother.

Sheriff Eichner was a hefty man with a large protruding belly, his shirt buttons strained. He wore a leather vest and badge. Sitting behind his desk with his feet up, he remained comfortable as Nathan entered. The lawman's face was round and chubby, his small eyes pale, a cigar in his teeth. He glared at Nathan, who sat down in front of his desk.

"Nathan Reed, Sheriff. I thought you'd like to know there's more Apaches out there on the move."

"That so? Well, the army takes care of that."

"Jose Chavez lost two men, but it may not have been Apaches. Maybe you'd want to ride out and have a look."

"It was Apaches, and I ain't got time for no Mexicans. I got enough work here to keep me busy day and night. And I don't reckon you got any call to come in here and tell me how to run my business."

Nathan pushed his hat back and considered the man. "'A fellow at the cantina told me an army major was murdered some time back. And a week ago, one of your deputies."

Eichner put his feet down and stood up. "Nobody knows who done it. Now why don't you go on your way?"

Nathan stood up slowly. Chavez was right about this man, but there was still another deputy. He turned and went to the door, then paused and looked back as he spoke.

"Any strangers around town?"

Eichner grunted. "Everyone's a stranger around here."

Nathan went outside just as the northbound stage rolled in with an armed guard of four men. The driver, and shotgun guard looked weary in their slickers, heads down, obviously worn from the worry of getting past the Mescaleros.

Nathan paused, then shook his head. Quincy would never ride a stagecoach. His friend was too much like him, a man who preferred the stars for his roof.

Chavez rode over with supplies loaded on his spare horse to say goodbye. "I have not been able to hire men, but I have asked my friends at the cantina to find someone for me."

"Good luck."

"You keep the black, Señor, as long as you need him."

"I'll buy him from you."

"I wish no money from you, Señor."

"Ten dollars?"

Chavez hesitated, then nodded, reaching inside his shirt. Shielding a store receipt from the rain, he wrote a bill of sale on the back with a pencil, then handed it over in exchange for the gold pieces Nathan offered.

Nathan thanked him and watched the Mexican rancher ride on up the street, just as three rowdy looking ranch-hands came out of a saloon. They were young, thin-faced, red-headed, intoxicated, and laughing until they saw Chavez passing.

"Hey, there's another Mex," said the skinny one with a white scar on his left cheek. "Hey, Mex, don't stick your nose up when you ride by."

Chavez ignored them. One of them, stocky with a big mustache, ran and grabbed his stirrup, jerking at his leg. Chavez's horse shied, but the man wouldn't let go.

"Get down. We wanna have some fun."

There were men along the street pausing to watch. Some were Mexicans. No one moved to interfere.

"I'm Trapper Corley, and them's my brothers, Brick and Slack, and we work for the Cromwells," the stocky one said.

31

"That means you gotta do what we say. Now get down from there."

Chavez glared down at him, then spat in his face.

Enraged, Trapper jumped up and grabbed Chavez's belt, jerking him half out of the saddle as his horse reared. The other youths came to help, one grabbing the reins. Chavez beat at them with his fist.

Suddenly, big hands from nowhere grabbed Trapper Corley by the back of the neck and belt, then lifted him in the air like a sack of flour, spun him like a top and threw him crashing over the railing and onto the boardwalk. Trapper landed hard and rolled up, gasping for air as Nathan turned to face the other two.

Slack, the skinny one, backed away, but Brick was a little taller, a lot bigger and a little braver, with a fatter nose. He had large shoulders and hands, and he was coming slowly forward, round face twisted, eyes bugging.

"I'm gonna tear you apart, stranger. Around here, we don't go standin' up for any Mexicans."

Nathan heard the click of a hammer, and he spun, six-gun springing into his hand. Sitting on the boardwalk, revolver aimed and his finger on the trigger, Trapper stared in amazement. He had never seen anyone draw that fast, and he realized Nathan was too dangerous to fight, at least right now when Trapper wasn't ready to die.

Nathan's six-gun was held with deadly aim, and Trapper hesitated, then numb with fear, put his left hand over his weapon and lowered it, releasing the hammer and shoving it back into his holster. His face was twisted with sudden defiance to put on a show for the onlookers.

Nathan holstered his six-gun and turned to the other two

brothers. Abruptly, the skinny one put his hand on the bigger one's arm and shook his head.

"Not now, Brick. Let's get him later. When we're sober."

Nathan stood quiet as the brothers helped Trapper to his feet and back into the saloon. Men who were along the street seemed to disappear, except for the Mexicans, who whispered to each other in hidden delight.

Chavez turned in the saddle. "I am indebted to you, Señor Reed."

Nathan walked over to stand next to him and spoke quietly. "There may come a time when I'll need your help."

"You need only to ask, Señor."

Nathan nodded farewell as the rancher rode on out of town. Then he heard a familiar deep chuckle and that same raspy voice.

"I heard a ruckus, and I figured it was you, Nathan."

"Quincy."

Nathan turned around. The short, stocky trapper was wearing buckskin and looking as if he just came out of the Shining Mountains. He had a grubby fur cap and carried his old Sharps. There was joy in his old gray eyes and a quiver to his silver mustache. This man had saved Nathan's life more than once.

"You came in on the stage?" Nathan asked, shaking bis hand. "How could they stand the smell of you?"

"I got me some real sweet toilet water."

"I thought that was skunk oil."

Quincy sobered. "I sure am glad to see you. Your letter was a real surprise."

"Let's hope it leads to somethin'."

Quincy would not settle for a handshake and hugged him

until Nathan could not breathe. Finally, Quincy drew back but kept his hands on Nathan's arms, fingers digging in deep, as if bracing him for some kind of blow.

"Well, first off, Nathan, I come up on the stage because of the armed guards, and there's a reason for wantin' that protection. Something I gotta tell you. Remember how I wrote you the Comancheros burned the house with your wife and your men inside? And that your son died with 'em? Well, I was wrong."

Stunned, Nathan stared at him, waiting.

And then he felt a tug at the back of his shirt, down around the fringe. He heard a small, plaintive voice behind him, a voice that sent a startled chill charging through him so fast, he nearly lost his balance.

"Pa?"

FOUR

*T*he small voice repeated the word anxiously.

"Pa?"

Nathan turned so slowly he could hear his every muscle straining. His heart was in his throat, and he stared down at a boy of about eleven in a store-bought suit with a face round and pink under a brimmed cap, eyes big and blue and full of tears as drizzling rain dampened his curly, sandy hair.

"My God," Nathan whispered, knees buckling.

"Pa, it's me, Timothy."

Nathan felt Quincy's big hands on his arms, holding him steady as he dropped to one knee and kept staring at the boy. Tears filled Nathan's eyes, and he felt cold sweat on his body. He could hardly breathe. His heart had stopped and now was drumming wildly. His voice was painful and sounded far away.

"Dear God, it's my son."

So cold and devastated he could hardly move, Nathan fought to bring up his big hands, for each hand suddenly weighed a ton. It was all he could do to reach for the boy, but when he did, he crushed him in his big arms, frantic he might disappear.

"Dear God. Thank you, God," he mumbled over and over.

Timothy's small arms went around Nathan's neck, and he hugged his father even as sobs wracked his slight frame.

Quincy knelt and spoke quietly. "Timothy was out at the barn playing when the Comancheros hit. There was nothing he could do, so he hid."

Nathan kept hugging and kissing his son as Quincy continued the story, and Timothy clung to his father. Emotion was throbbing between them.

"Some young Comanche rode into the barn and saw Timothy. He waited until the others rode off, then took the boy to Charo, a branch of Quanah Parker's band. You know Quanah had taken his people to Fort Sill back in '75, but Charo had split off and stayed runnin' wild. I recollect his best time was chasin' trains to scare the passengers. And emptyin' the water tanks. He wasn't killin', just harrassin'.

"Anyhow, Charo took care of Timothy but never turned him in because he was hidin' out from the army. But he liked the boy. About two months ago I heard he had a captive.

"Me and Quanah, we go back a long way, and I knew Charo, so I tracked him down and traded for the boy. You was already on your way, so I just brought him along. Figured the stage was safer. And here he is."

Timothy was hugging Nathan, fingers digging into his back as he sobbed. Nathan held him tight, kissing his sandy hair. This was his son, back from the dead. He gave thanks over and over. But deep in his joy was the realization his son had been forced to watch his mother die in the fire.

"Pa, you never came for me," the boy murmured.

"I didn't know, son. I didn't know."

"I prayed and prayed, and nobody came."

"Quincy came," Nathan said, tears and rain trickling down his face as he held him back a little. "Let me look at you, son. You're so tall. Eleven years old. And good and healthy. Don't seem like Charo beat on you much."

"They was teaching me a lot, and they was good to me, but I was scared the Comancheros would find out I was alive and come after me to shut me up. But I can't remember their faces anyhow, Pa. It's all gone. Quincy says I blocked it out."

Nathan looked at Quincy, who was sniffing back his tears, and he nodded as he hugged his son again.

"Thanks, Quincy."

"Let's get a room at the hotel, Nathan."

"Pa, Quincy said you had the Sioux runnin' scared. And you chased the Chiricahuas into Mexico. And General Crook can't never do nothin' without you."

"Well, Quincy dresses things up a little."

Timothy was grinning, his hand in Nathan's.

After a hearty meal at a cafe near the courthouse, they retired from the rain in a second floor hotel room that overlooked the street. There was a big glass window that opened like a door to the balcony.

Nathan could not get enough of his son. He kept touching him, hugging him, looking at him constantly. The feeling was mutual.

Nathan sat on the edge of the bed, his hand on his son's shoulder. He had tried to be calm, to accept that his son was safe and life could continue.

But Nathan pulled Timothy into his arms, tears filling his eyes again. Three hands and his wife had died in the ranch house fire, and another man in the field, but Timothy was here, alive, smiling, warm to the touch, little fingers twisting in the fringe of his jacket. Nathan wept, and so did Quincy.

"Son, I sure would like to meet that young Comanche that helped you get away."

"He's stayed with Charo. He was always playing jokes on the others. He was very funny. Maybe we could go back there someday? If we can find them."

"Sure, son."

Son, Nathan thought. The word was like velvet on his tongue. Later when Timothy slept, moaning in his sleep with his fingers tight in the fringe of Nathan's shirt, Quincy wiped his eyes with the back of his hand.

"Nathan, that boy has nightmares all the time. He knew his Ma and the others were trapped in the house, and he probably relives it in his dreams, even if he's blocked most of it out when he's awake."

"I tell you, Quincy, seein' my son, I can't thank you enough. But I'm right worried. Would Wolf know who he is?"

"The way Wolf and his army were raiding, ain't likely he knew the names of anybody he rode over."

"I sure hope you're right."

"You know, about the time Wolf raided your place, he got some gold off an army wagon. Near Fort McIntosh, down by Laredo. He just disappeared after he hit your place and a couple others. But you got to know, even when the army quit lookin', I was out there, Nathan."

"I know, Quincy."

"Now that letter you sent, askin' me to meet you here because you saw an army news dispatch. About how a Mexican was killed near Black River with a 'W' carved on his forehead. That was a real surprise. Maybe Wolf couldn't help hisself, or could be that's what he wants. To keep the fear alive."

Nathan was grim. "Well, don't tell Timothy unless we have to. Charo know anything about Wolf?"

"He knew of 'im, but he'd never seen 'im. And you now Quanah, he'd have no dealin's with Comancheros."

"Well, I ain't never going to rest until I find Wolf."

"You ever find 'im, I'll tell you this, he won't be easy to take."

"I'll take 'im. But I got to tell you, Quincy, when we stopped at the fort, some feller named Beeler tried to knife me out in the stable. Seems he and his father supplied cattle for the Cromwells' outfit."

"Why'd he wanna kill you?"

"That's what I'd like to know. But I don't think it has anything to do with Wolf. You and me, and General Crook, we're the only ones know why we're here."

"And you never saw this Beeler before?"

"No, but Captain Paine seems to think Crook sent me here for some other reason, maybe to check on 'im. He was mighty nervous about it. Oakley figured Paine's in some kind of thievin' with Cromwell, so they could have paid Beeler. But I'll just go on lettin' 'em think it. Makes a good cover."

"What are you goin' to tell Timothy?"

"Maybe just that, that Crook sent us here to check out Paine and Cromwell. I don't want to frighten the boy. He's had enough. But we got to stick around until Wolf tips his hand."

"He's an animal. They don't stay quiet long."

Chills running down his back, Nathan felt anxiety cutting him like a knife. Hatred for Wolf had been smoldering in him for the last two years, ever since he received Quincy's year-old letter, but it was a hatred that could never be erased by inaction. Nathan felt he could kill the man with his bare hands.

But right now, Nathan had Timothy, safe and asleep and close to him. He wiped his eyes with the back of his hand.

"Quincy, I can never repay you for finding my son."

And while Nathan talked with Quincy, Captain Paine was driving his buggy up in front of the Cromwells' fine house on a high slope at the east end of town. It was still drizzling, and Leslie shivered under the slicker she was wearing over her dress. Chavez's floppy hat still protected her face and hair. Paine, also in a slicker, came around to help her down on the boardwalk.

There was a wooden walk up to the front door, avoiding the mud. Paine led the way and pounded on the big walnut door. Lupe, the Mexican housemaid, looked them over, then let them inside and helped Leslie remove her slicker.

Paine bid Leslie sit down on a stuffed chair in the parlor while he went to find Jason. Lupe disappeared.

She gazed around the ornate room. Jason had a lot of money, and he had let her know that many times, even when she was on Paul's arm. He would be pressuring her to marry, but all of her instincts told her to wait, to be careful.

Nathan had stirred new emotions within her, but she had to believe she had only been grateful. Besides, Nathan had memories he could never escape and would likely never love again. Still, he had become her hero.

Suddenly, Jason Cromwell came hurrying around the

comer, then stopped abruptly to stare at her. He was wearing a quilted smoking jacket. Behind him was Rachet, followed by Paine.

Jason was stockier than Paul had been, his face sagging at little, his dark, searing eyes round under thick, heavy eyebrows. He had receding brown hair and a mole on his left cheek. His mouth was wide, and he flashed big white teeth. He was maybe in his mid-forties, and he had a commanding presence. But she had forgotten about the fierceness always gleaming in his gaze, even when he smiled. His eyes had a life of their own.

"Leslie. I just heard about the wagons. I'm so glad you're all right."

He took her hand in his and bowed to kiss her fingers.

Paine stiffened. "I gave Mrs. Cromwell my quarters last night. And I arranged for some clothes for her."

"Thanks, Captain. Now she will be my guest."

Leslie felt uncomfortable but she had no money for the hotel. She had nothing of her own. Jason was overpowering, and he drew her to her feet as he called for Lupe.

"My brother Titus, he'll be glad you're safe as well."

"Titus is here?" she asked, uneasy.

"He's delivering goods right now. But he'll be back. Now you must be tired. Lupe will show you to your room. You get some rest, and then tomorrow, Lupe will take you shopping."

"It's not necessary, Jason."

"Nothing is too good for Paul's widow."

As Leslie was led away by the small housekeeper, Jason moistened his lips, watching her up the stairs and out of sight. He drew a deep breath and wiped his lined brow with the back of his hand.

41

"I'm going to marry her."

Paine frowned. "I was thinking the same thing."

"I didn't bring her up here for you."

Rachet interrupted. "We got to talk, Jason."

The three men retreated to Jason's study where he sat behind his big fancy walnut desk and lit his pipe. Behind him was an ornate rack with white Stetsons and silk bandannas. The lamps were solid brass, the drapes were green velvet.

Paine took a cigar but didn't light it, his mind on Leslie, but Rachet was on the edge of his chair.

"It's the books again. We was payin' Beeler five dollars a head for stolen beef, and we been sellin' to the government at a dollar sixty-three a pound just to undercut Chisum. That's cuttin' us mighty thin. And we can't keep stretching what we don't have. Plus I can't invent any more Mescaleros to feed. As it is, you'll soon be broke."

"Don't worry," Jason said, leaning back. "My brother Titus and I have reserves. Just do your best. Now what about my wagons? That second train get through?"

"Haven't seen it," Rachet said.

"You get some of the boys to ride out and meet it. I'm plenty fed up with Victorio."

"If you hadn't framed him for murder," Paine said, "he wouldn't be so damed mad. When that fool private played that bugle outside the reservation, Victorio knew we were coming. He took off, and I can tell you this, New Mexico Territory is going to suffer."

"As long as I don't," Jason said.

"If the army starts investigating me," Paine replied, "I'm not going down alone."

"You get your share," Jason said, "but you keep gambling it away."

Paine made a face and leaned back in his chair, biting the end of his cigar. "You had that last investigator killed. I had no part in that."

Rachet grunted. "We made it look like an accident. Horse run away with him, that's all."

"Then you had the major killed," Paine added.

"Some town drunk must have done it," Jason said with a smile. "Besides, he was on to you. He told the sheriff about it. Which was a big mistake. So we did you a favor."

Paine frowned. "Maybe, but all this killing will bring nothing but trouble from the outside. Your men got that deputy who was gettin' suspicious. And you got all the other traders mad at you. You can't ride roughshod over the whole town forever, Jason."

"Nobody has the guts to stop me."

Paine toyed with the cigar. "When Leslie got to the fort, she was with Nathan Reed. Now I heard about him. He was a personal scout for General Crook. So what's he doin' here? I think he was sent to investigate."

"I was way ahead of you," Rachet said. "Some of the men recognized him. So I sent that fool Beeler out to kill 'im while we had the opportunity."

"That fool got himself killed," Paine snapped. "If you want to get rid of Reed, you got to do better than trying to knife him in a barn right in the middle of my army post. And with a witness, no less."

"Beeler was gonna get 'em both," Rachet snapped.

Jason was looking from one to the other. "What's all this about Nathan Reed?"

"Well," Paine said, "we figure he was sent here undercover to try to get evidence on what we're doing. So we got to get rid of him."

Jason grunted. "If Heeler's dead, his Pa is gonna come gunning for Reed hisself. We may not have to do anything."

"All this talk," Rachet said, "don't accomplish nothing. I tell you, I ain't goin' to prison. Reed has got to die."

"No," Jason said. "One nosy investigator dead by accident, we can get away with. One major, that can happen anywhere, and Paine covered that up. Nobody cares about the deputy. But another dead investigator, especially one from General Crook, that would just bring the whole federal government and half the army down on us. If Beeler don't get him, let him nose around. Just make sure he don't find anything."

Paine grunted. "That attack at the post must've given Reed some idea we're on to him."

"I say kill 'im," Rachet insisted. "And that other deputy, this Dooley, we got to get rid of him."

Paine shook his head. "He's a kid. A nothing."

"Well, Reed ain't," Rachet said. "He's dangerous."

Paine and Rachet got ready to leave, but Rachet lingered as Paine went out to the buggy. The thin man was grinning.

"Paine buys it all. If he knew we was gettin' rich, he'd sure be mad."

"We need him, so be careful."

Rachet left, and Jason leaned back in his chair, puffing on his pipe and smiling to himself. Upstairs was the woman he was going to marry. At last. And no one, not even this Nathan Reed, was going to get in his way.

Out in the street of Black River, Nathan and Quincy were

taking Timothy down to the store for some clothes. Nathan allowed as how he could use a new outfit himself. It was cold and drizzling, the sky gray and ominous.

"I didn't buy this suit," Timothy said. "It was the ladies what took care of me when Quincy brung me in."

Quincy grinned. "Well, the ladies were sure fussin' over him. I couldn't hurt their feelin's."

When they came out of the store, Timothy was wearing wool britches, a plaid wool shirt under a leather jacket, and a small slicker. He had a small, wide-brimmed hat and looked like a miniature cowhand. He carried a bundle of other clothes. Nathan was so proud he was busting his buttons.

And Nathan had a new blue, double-breasted shirt, black leather vest, and wool britches. He had a new leather jacket with fringe, its pockets full of boxes of shells. Rain dribbled off his wide-brimmed Stetson.

The wet boardwalk creaked and sagged under their boots. Timothy held his father's hand, which he constantly found close to him, and he gazed up at Nathan with a grin.

"I look just like you, Pa."

"Well, not quite, but you'll do."

The sheriff suddenly came out of his office and crossed over the muddy street to confront them, his fat belly moving up and down. "Listen here, Reed. I just had a complaint about you."

"That so?"

"You assaulted Trapper Corley."

"He was attacking Chavez. I had a right to step in."

"Chavez is a lousy Mexican."

"This was their country, you know."

"Sure, and it was the Mescaleros' before 'em, wasn't it? Well, we're here now, and we don't take sides against Americans."

"Chavez is an American now."

"Blast you, Reed. You ain't listenin'."

The sheriff ranted and raved for about ten minutes while Nathan stood his ground. Then the lawman stormed off, and Timothy's face was full of pride. He held his father's hand tight as they returned to the hotel.

"We're going to eat in the dining room tonight," Nathan told his son. "Just like city folks."

But when they walked through the plush lobby and entered the dining room, Nathan came to a halt. Leslie was sitting at a window table with Captain Paine and a stocky man he took to be a Cromwell.

Leslie was staring at the boy, and she stood up, walking over to meet them. "Nathan?"

He swallowed hard. "This is my son Timothy. He wasn't dead after all. He was with the Comanches, and Quincy here got 'im back."

Tears came to her eyes. "Oh, Nathan—"

She choked on her words and suddenly knelt in front of Timothy, who while clutching his father's hand, cautiously shook hers. Nathan was trembling, sharing her joy.

"Timothy," she said, rising slowly. "Dear God, Nathan."

Nathan was choking on his emotions, fighting not to let the tears come. Abruptly, she moved forward and hugged Nathan, her face at his chest. His arms went around her, and he held her tight, a sob going through him. His fingers dug in the thickness of her shining hair. Then she slid from his embrace and looked down at Timothy.

"Timothy," she said, "your father saved me from the Apaches. He's a brave man."

Jason came over to take her arm. "Mrs. Cromwell, you've forgotten your station."

Nathan frowned. "I take it you're Jason Cromwell?"

"That's right. And I suppose you're Nathan Reed. The Captain tells me you brought Mrs. Cromwell to the fort. For that I am grateful, but I'll thank you to leave her be. The Cromwells have position in this community."

Before Nathan could react, Leslie stiffened and turned to glare at Jason, her dark eyes flashing.

"Excuse me, Jason, but this man saved my life."

Jason looked from her to the stately Nathan and the stem little boy. Jason's searing eyes were like hot coals in the false aristocracy of his face and manner. He looked the scraggly Quincy over with disdain. Then he looked again at the boy, this time studying him. Timothy glared back at him.

Jason looked at Leslie, her lovely face set with anxiety, and he realized he was alienating her. He drew himself up and took her hand.

"Very well, Leslie," Jason said, grimly. "Thank him if you must. I'll even pay him. But come back to supper."

She hesitated, then suddenly knelt and drew Timothy into her arms, hugging him. He hugged her back. For a long moment, she just held the boy tight with affection. When she let go, Timothy held on, and when he let go, she didn't want to release him. She kissed his cheek.

"God bless you, Timothy," she whispered.

She finally withdrew and slowly stood up, smiled at Nathan with tears in her eyes, and turned to walk back with the angry

Jason Cromwell, who glared over his shoulder.

Timothy watched her sit down with Jason. "I like her, Pa, but I sure don't like him. He's got funny eyes."

Quincy made a face. "All of a sudden, I ain't so hungry."

"We'll go to the cafe," Nathan said. "Over by the courthouse."

When they were gone, Jason leaned against the table to put his hand on Leslie's. "You mustn't forget yourself like that. The Cromwell name is very highly regarded in Black River. If you step down with the peasants, you become one."

"Jason, I told you. Nathan Reed saved my life."

"You want me to give him money?"

She stared at him, then shook her head. Jason leaned back, studying her before smiling and trying to make small talk. But she had seen something in Jason she did not like, and she had never felt so lonely nor so trapped.

Captain Paine tried hard for her attention, and she knew both these men would give her no rest. On the frontier, single women were hard to find. Jason had wanted her at first sight in Mesilla, even when he knew she was to marry his brother, and now he would be persistent.

There had been times she had even feared Jason had killed his own brother on her wedding day, just to have her for himself. But she had discounted her fears, telling herself she was not that wonderful a prize.

Later that night, Leslie went to her room, followed by Lupe, who paused just inside the door and whispered.

"Señora, I'm am worried for you."

"What is it, Lupe?"

"Señor Jason. He is a strange man."

"What do you mean?"

"Sometimes, I think he is two men. One smiles and goes to the town. The other walks at night in the garden, talking to himself and making noises. One night I saw him slashing at a tree with his knife."

"Maybe he just can't sleep."

"I think you should go to the boarding house."

"But I have no money, Lupe."

The older woman frowned, nodded and went out of the room, closing the door behind her and leaving Leslie so frightened she could not sleep.

While she tossed and turned, Paine and Jason went into the study. Paine was chattering about how lovely Leslie was and how all was fair in love and war. The officer didn't see the fury in Jason's face until Jason slammed his fist on his desk.

Paine was unnerved. "Look, Jason, let her decide."

But Jason hadn't heard anything Paine had said. He was still thinking of Nathan's encounter with Leslie at the hotel. He had been furious when she had hugged Nathan and his boy. His jealousy had been hot lava in his belly.

And now he was livid, red flashes of color in his face.

"I changed my mind. I want Nathan Reed dead. Now."

FIVE

In the morning, the sun was shining despite moving clouds, but the streets were still muddy. Nathan and Quincy made plans in their room as Timothy slept on the bed against the wall.

Nathan pulled on his boots. "We'll split up, Quincy. You go on out to the fort. Find Private Oakley. He'll be glad to help us if he knows anything. I don't see him connected with Cromwells' doin's. I think you can trust him."

"All right."

"You might ride on out to see Chavez. He's in the clear as far as I can see. You oughta be able to fill him in, and he might be able to help. He seems to know everything that goes on around here. Me and Timothy, we'll meet up with the deputy that's still alive. So far, I get the story he's not on Cromwell's payroll."

"You be careful, Nathan."

"We'll let Timothy think we are investigating the Cromwells' dealin's with the army. I don't want him losin' any sleep over the fact Wolf might be around here."

The deputy was found at the cafe just down the street, having breakfast by himself. He was in his early twenties, lean and hard, with a fresh but ruddy face. He was wearing a leather vest on which he wore his star. There were only four other men in the small room, which had only a dozen tables. A rosy-faced little woman was serving.

Nathan and Timothy approached.

"Mind if we join you?"

The deputy looked up, startled. "Oh, sure."

Timothy sat between them, and Nathan sized the man up as best he could as they shook hands. The deputy had a good strong grip and a friendly smile.

"I'm Nathan Reed. My son, Timothy."

"Mike Dooley."

They ordered breakfast, and Nathan kept the conversation light until he settled back with his coffee.

"I heard the other deputy was killed. You figure who done it?"

"No tellin'. Death comes cheap around here."

Jason sipped his coffee. "Your sheriff wasn't too friendly yesterday."

"He has a short rein all right."

"My boy and I, we're thinkin' of settling around here."

"If you're lookin' for land, there ain't any. The Cromwells and some of the others have it all staked out. Unless you want prairie sand."

"Maybe some of them would sell."

"Not the Cromwells. But you can try the small ranchers. Some are fed up. And you could probably buy a tradin' company right cheap about now. Cromwell has the army and reservation business all sewed up."

"You from around here, Mike?"

"Nope. I'm from Missouri. Got family back there. But I figured I wasn't cut out to be no farmer. I like wearin' a badge. Got here three months ago. I'd heard how rough it was in New Mexico Territory. All the lawlessness, especially over in Lincoln. But Black River turned out to be a lot worse."

It was then that the other men in the cantina began to stand up and move to the back and other side of the room. Nathan, his back to the wall, turned his gaze slowly toward the door.

Moving inside were the three Corley brothers. The bigger one, Brick, was in front and coming toward them, a sneer on his face, his hand resting on his holster.

"What's going on?" Dooley asked.

"Pa shamed 'em," Timothy said.

Brick loomed big and mean looking over the table. "Reed, we got business with you."

"Seems to me we finished."

"We was drunk. We ain't now."

Dooley leaned back in his chair. "You men move along."

Brick ignored the deputy. "Outside, Reed. Unless you want it in here."

Dooley stood up, six-gun in hand. "I said, move along."

Brick was startled, obviously never expecting the young deputy to have any sand. "You're new around here, Dooley. We work for Jason Cromwell and his brother."

"That don't cut no ice. Now move."

Brick drew himself up, eyes blazing. "All right, Reed, we'll get you later. I'm gonna bust your bones. And you, deputy, wait 'til Jason hears about this."

The angry brothers turned and stormed out of the cantina.

Dooley holstered his six-gun and sat down to take up his coffee, shaking his head.

"They're a bad bunch."

Nathan sipped his coffee. "Only as mean as the man what pays 'em."

Timothy looked at his father with so much pride, Nathan felt his heart swell. And Nathan hated himself for not having been home to enjoy a son like this. He remembered taking Timothy fishing when the boy was eight. Maybe they would do that again.

They finished their breakfast and walked out into the sunlight that was peering through the clouds. There was no sign of the Corleys. But coming out of the store across the street were Leslie and the Mexican housekeeper.

"Handsome woman," Dooley said. "I hear Jason's already set to marry her. Too bad."

Nathan hesitated. Lupe was lifting her skirt with one hand and carrying packages with the other as she started across through the mud. Leslie was balancing a package with one hand and lifting her skirts with the other. She was wearing a green dress and white cape, her shining hair spread on her shoulders, and she looked wonderful.

Nathan couldn't resist. "You stay here, son."

The deputy and Timothy stood quiet as Nathan walked across the muddy street toward the women. He nodded to the little Spanish housekeeper who was crossing alone, holding her skirts above the mud and swaying unsteadily. He caught her arm, and she leaned close.

"Señor, you must get her out of that house."

"What's wrong?"

"Please, get her out. There is a nice boarding house, over by the school. And there is no teacher anymore. Please, talk to the mayor, Señor Crutchfield. He is in the courthouse."

Nathan squeezed her arm as she continued past him.

Leslie was still on the boardwalk. When she saw Nathan coming, she brightened, letting her skirts fall softly about her. He stepped out of the mud and onto the creaking boards.

"Need a lift?" Nathan asked.

Beaming, she smiled. "Nathan, I'm so glad to see you. How is your son?"

"I'm right proud, and that's a fact."

Tears brimmed in her eyes. "I gave thanks last night that you found him."

"So did I."

Then she frowned. "I have to talk to you about Jason."

He reached for her, and she willingly folded as he lifted her in his arms. Her soft warmth in his grip was enough to make his face bum. She rested against him as he started into the muddy street, and in the middle, she stopped him. Her hand was resting on his chest.

"No one can hear us out here, Nathan."

"Jason bothering you?"

"He had a meeting with that Captain Paine and Mr. Rachet. There's something bad going on, Nathan."

"You stay out of it. It could be dangerous."

"And this morning, that Rachet was there again. I overheard them say something about you being a government agent. Is it true?"

Nathan held her a little closer. "No, but let 'em think it. It'll keep 'em busy."

"His brother Titus is here somewhere, and that worries me, Nathan. I'm afraid of Titus."

"Maybe you ought to move into the boarding house."

"I have no money. I don't even have clothes except what Jason has just bought me."

Nathan turned around in the mud and headed toward the courthouse, Timothy and Lupe following. Leslie clung to him in surprise. Inside, the fat, puff-faced mayor was delighted to hire her as the town teacher.

"We can have the children gathered up in a week," he said, cheerfully. "And my wife runs the boarding house, so you'll have no problem getting a room."

Next, Leslie's hand in his, Timothy and Lupe still following, Nathan led her to the boarding house near the little school and arranged a room with the pert and pinch-faced Mrs. Crutchfield.

Lupe hauled the packages to Leslie's small upstairs room while the others went onto the porch as rain began to drizzle once more, the sun having disappeared behind the darkening clouds.

Leslie was still in a daze. "But I still can't pay Jason for these clothes. And I won't be paid as teacher for another two weeks."

"I'll be payin' you to take care of my son whenever I have to ride out of town."

"I could never take money for that."

"It'd pay your rent."

"All right, just until I'm paid as a teacher, but what does Timothy say about it?"

Nathan cleared his throat. "I got business here, son. I may have to leave you on your own now and then. Leslie's going to look after you. Is that agreeable?"

"She's real pretty, Pa, but I want to go with you. I can ride and shoot as good as anyone."

Leslie leaned down toward Timothy. "Maybe I'm the one who needs looking after. Besides, you need to learn your letters."

"I ain't goin' to school."

"It's school, or tutorin'," Nathan said.

Leslie laughed softly. "Timothy, your father can read and write quite well. Don't you want to be like him?"

They stood in the shelter of the porch as the boy looked at her curiously. Nathan put his hand on his son's shoulder. The boy shrugged.

"All right, Pa."

And suddenly a rifle cracked.

The bullet knocked the brim of Nathan's hat upward. He spun, six-gun in hand, but saw no one. He shoved Leslie and Timothy down. The rifle cracked again, the bullet skimming his jacket.

Dooley came running back up the boardwalk on the other side of the street, looking in alleys, then crossing over.

Leslie had seized Timothy and pulled him into her arms where she knelt. Nathan turned quickly, his heart wild.

"Get inside, fast."

"But, Pa—"

The boy's face was colorless, his eyes wide as Leslie dragged him inside the boarding house.

Dooley and Nathan stood alone in the street as the rain became heavier. They looked around with piercing gaze. Dooley shook his head.

"He's long gone."

"I'm gonna have a look."

The two men cut across the empty street, boots sucking mud, rain covering them. The stores were silent, but there were faces peering from behind the curtains. Nathan went to the right, and Dooley to the left, each entering an alley at a run.

They came out the back between the buildings and saw nothing. They ran behind the hotel and stores, slipping and sliding on the mud. Pausing, breathing hard, they looked around with six-guns ready. Dooley frowned, biting his lip.

"That's the way it happens around here. Hit and run. And no sign of who done it. You were plenty lucky, Nathan."

"Whoever it was is gonna pay, shootin' at me with my son and Leslie right there."

"Got any idea who it was?"

Nathan frowned. "That man Beeler I had to kill at the fort. Maybe that wasn't the end of it. And I hear he has a father."

"Meanest old rat in the county, you can bet on it."

They walked around most of the buildings, but the rain covered any signs. Back on the boardwalk, Nathan glanced toward the sheriff's office. The man was sitting in there with his feet on his desk, ignoring the shots and taking life easy.

It was then that Dooley and Nathan turned in surprise as a dozen black cavalrymen came riding up the street from the east. Their horses were tired, heads down, legs barely moving. Their slickers were battered and thin.

The big man in the lead had a hard face and a broken nose, and he turned to ride toward them.

"I heard about them," Dooley said. "They been after Victorio but way south. Wonder why they're here."

The man reined up. "Deputy, I'm Sergeant Smith. You reckon we're headed for Fort Royale?"

"Yep."

"We been assigned there. Is it far?"

Dooley shook his head. "Just keep ridin' the way you're goin'. Maybe a couple hours, that's all. I'm Dooley. This here's Nathan Reed."

The sergeant straightened. "Nathan Reed? With General Crook?"

"Not anymore," Nathan said.

"We heard about you. You're kind of a legend."

"So are you and your men. Aren't you with the 9th?"

"We was, but seems the army thinks we're needed out of Fort Royale. The Apaches are everywhere now."

The sergeant adjusted his slicker, pulled his hat down tight, and headed back to his men and toward the west end of town.

"They don't have it easy," Nathan said. "War's barely fifteen years behind us. Mostly, they don't get good equipment. But their desertion level is lower than the rest. And they're good fighters."

"Paine ain't gonna like it," Dooley said. "His folks was from the south."

Nathan left him and headed back over to the boarding house where Timothy, Leslie and Lupe were waiting on the steps. Timothy came running to his father, hugging him.

"Pa, why'd they shoot at you?"

Nathan swallowed and looked at Leslie's pale face.

"Your father was probably mistaken for someone else," she said. "But tell me, Nathan, do I start work now?"

"Sure enough. Three dollars anytime you look after Timothy. Fair enough?"

Her eyes widened. "More than fair."

Nathan turned to the housekeeper. "Jason may take this out on you."

"I am paid well, and I am saving it. Also, I am not afraid of Señor Cromwell."

"Where would you go if you had to leave?"

"I do not know, Señor."

"Maybe you would marry Jose Chavez."

Lupe lifted her chin a little. "That dirty little man?"

"You like him, don't you?"

She smiled. "Maybe."

Lupe turned and left, but Leslie was worried.

"Jason will be furious when he finds I'm gone."

Timothy took her hand. "Don't worry, Leslie, I'll look after you."

While Nathan talked to her and his son in front of the boarding house, Jason Cromwell was seated at his desk in his fine house, shuffling papers and chewing on his pipe.

Seated in front of his desk was a large man who looked liked Jason, but who sported a short, trim black beard. He was younger, stockier, with big shoulders and hands, his eyes lighter brown but under the same heavy brows.

Jason leaned back. "Well, Titus, I'm sure glad you're back."

"The men are at the livery now, takin' care of the horses. They'll be unloadin' over at the warehouse. We brought in plenty of com."

"Business has been good, although Paine thinks it's rotten. We got most of the gold melted down. Things are looking up, Titus. And I'd say along about Christmas, I'll be getting married. I can use some extra to take her on a honeymoon somewhere."

"You, Jason? You gettin' married?"

"It's not funny."

Titus grinned, his beard twitching. "But you're pushin' fifty. Let us young ones handle the women. You just sit in your rocker."

"You don't worry about me. Any man married to Leslie will be young for a mighty long time."

Titus leaned forward, mouth twisted. "Leslie?"

"After Paul was killed, I sent for her."

"You asked her yet?"

"No, but I will."

"Well, listen to me, Jason, I got a yen for that woman. Who says you got first right?"

"You've become an animal. Why would she even look at you?"

"She looked at me, down in Mesilla. I know she had the same feelin's. And who are you to call me an animal? Maybe I act like one, but you are one, or are you forgettin' about Texas so easy in your fine smokin' jacket?"

Jason frowned. "You're loco. But you might be interested to know that Paine is after her as well."

"Paine?"

"Yes, him with his fancy uniform."

"So where is she?"

Jason told the story of her rescue, and Titus drew himself up like a bear. Jason rather enjoyed his brother's growl when he heard Reed's name.

"Jason, I heard about him. Why you figure he's here?"

"I would think the army sent him."

"You gonna kill 'im?"

"We're working on it. And Dooley may have to go." He

looked at the wall clock. "But right now, I'm wondering where she is. I sent her shopping, since she lost everything with the wagons."

They heard the front door, and both men jumped up, hurrying out of the den and into the parlor, pausing to see the housekeeper removing her cape.

"Lupe, where is she?" Jason demanded.

The woman replied that Leslie had moved into the boarding house. "Mr. Reed helped her. She is going to be the schoolteacher." Lupe then quickly went to her room. Jason was livid.

Titus grinned. "So she's gonna marry you, eh? So why did she move out?"

"She must think it's more proper, that's all."

"Yeah, well, I'll bet Nathan Reed wants her for hisself."

Jason's face darkened with anger and frustration, his wild eyes ablaze, and then he spun on his heel and went back to his den, Titus following with a bellowing laugh.

While the brothers argued, Leslie had happily moved into her room and showed *Nathan* her new riding outfit in one of the packages. Timothy went to the glass window that served as a door to the balcony. Nathan stood with hat in hand. The boy pushed the curtains away and moved the glass aside.

"You got a balcony just like us. Except yours is all little and private, and we got the big one all across the front of the hotel. But you got a big tree outside yours."

Nathan was feeling rather awkward. "You keep your doors locked. Now, tomorrow mornin', I'm ridin' out to meet up with Quincy."

"Can I go with you, Pa?"

"Someone's tryin' to kill me, son. I don't want you hurt."

Timothy pleaded, but to no avail. It was then that Quincy appeared in the open doorway, water dribbling off his slicker, and Nathan knew something was wrong.

"Quincy, what's happened?"

"Dooley told me where you was. They found Chavez's men."

From the strange look on Quincy's face, Nathan knew even more. "Timothy, you stay here with Leslie. I have to talk with Quincy."

"Aw, Pa."

Nathan squeezed the boy's shoulder and went into the hallway with Quincy, closing the door behind him. Quincy led the way downstairs and out onto the porch where they stood protected from the rain. It was a long moment before Quincy could speak.

"Nathan, I rode out to Chavez's to talk with him, see what he knew. The army had brought the bodies to his ranch."

"And?"

Quincy swallowed. "There was a W carved on the forehead of one and the back of another. And Chavez said they even took a gold watch from one of 'em. Had the man's father's name on it. Roberto Sanchez. If we could just find someone with that watch."

"So Wolf really is here."

"Either that, or someone's tryin' to put the blame on him."

Nathan's hands turned into fists. "He's here. I can feel it."

"I had to tell Chavez, but I didn't tell the army."

"Chavez is all right."

"There's something else, Nathan."

SIX

*Q*uincy leaned on the porch post, staring out at the rain as he removed his hat and shook the wet from the brim.

"What is it, Quincy?"

"At the fort, Oakley showed me that Rachet fellow. And I was sure I'd seen him afore. As I was riding into town, it come to me. I seen him in Texas. In jail."

"In jail?"

"The rangers caught him sellin' whiskey and guns to the Comanches."

Nathan felt cold and turned grim. "You think he was involved with the Comancheros?"

"Well, as I remember it, they found him and his wagon in a canyon with a half dozen Comanches, and the army moved in on 'em. Three braves were killed and the others got away. Rode right up the canyon wall. You know them Comanches. Best horsemen in the country."

"So maybe he wasn't sellin' to 'em. Maybe he was workin' with 'em. Supplyin' 'em."

"That's what I figure. But he convinced them he was just movin' his supplies and the Comanches surrounded him and he was too scared not to trade. So the army let him off."

"You think he's Wolf?"

Quincy shook his head. "He's a mean little man all right, but he's all coward. The way I see this Wolf, he ain't afraid of nothin'. In fact, I figure Wolf thinks he's indestructible."

Nathan slammed his right fist into his left palm. "Blast it, Quincy. When I come here, it was to take revenge. But now it's more than that. We've got to stop him."

"But there can't be that many strangers in town."

"He don't have to be a stranger, Quincy. Remember, it's been three years since Wolf disappeared. And these killin' s with his mark just started six months ago. Wolf could have been here all this time and just went back to his old ways."

"There's somethin' else, Nathan. Oakley says everyone's certain you're a government agent."

"That's good. I don't want Wolf to know we're lookin' for 'im."

Quincy nodded, and they went back into the lobby of the boarding house as Leslie and Timothy came down the stairs. The boy hurried to his father, who took their slickers from the wall hook.

"What is it, Pa?"

"Son, like I told you, Quincy and me, we're lookin' into things for the federal government. And he's been out askin' questions. That's all."

Timothy looked at Quincy, unconvinced.

"Hey, Timothy," Quincy said, abruptly, "they got some of that striped candy over at the store across the street. How about you and me goin' over and pickin' some out?"

"Can I, Pa?"

Nathan grinned. "Sure, son. We'll wait here."

Quincy pulled the boy's slicker back on him, and they headed into the rain and across the street. Nathan and Leslie stood on the porch, watching them go into the store.

Leslie leaned on a post and turned to look at Nathan, who was standing rather close. Her dark blue eyes were round and shining with the threat of tears.

"It must have been terrible for Timothy. Seeing his mother die that way. And you, Nathan, you're still grieving for her."

He was grim, but talking with Leslie gave him peace.

"I think of her all the time. She was small with yellow hair. She laughed a lot. And she never once said I shouldn't go where General Crook ordered. But I should have been there."

"You can't be everywhere at the same time, Nathan."

"What about you and Paul Cromwell? You miss him?"

She stared out at the rain. "I hardly knew him, and we were never really man and wife before he died, but he was a nice man. I think I miss what might have been."

"Well, at least you're away from his brothers."

She turned slowly. "Nathan, why are you really here?"

"It's a dangerous thing to know."

"But you can trust me, Nathan. You saved my life." He swallowed. "I'm after Wolf."

"The man who killed your wife?"

"Yes. He's leaving his mark around here."

"What do you mean?"

"He carves the initial W on his victims. One man was found that way some months ago. And now Chavez's men."

"Oh, Nathan."

"He's here, Leslie. I've got to find him. Don't let anyone know why I'm here. And I sure don't want Timothy to know. He's been through enough."

"Does this Wolf know who Timothy is?"

"No, Timothy was hiding in the barn during the raid. And it ain't likely Wolf even knew whose place he was raiding. They were just wiping out the countryside and anything in their path."

"Would Timothy recognize him?"

"Not likely. Besides, he's blocked it all out."

She looked terribly sad, and tears brimmed in her eyes. She slowly straightened and moved toward him. He turned to face her. She was within inches of him now.

Abruptly, she slid into his embrace. He held her tight, his face against her soft, lustrous hair. She felt warm and yielding against him. He told himself she was only worried about Timothy and feeling sorry for Nathan. It was just as well, because the memory of his wife was controlling his every thought.

As he held her even closer, he glanced through the rain, and he saw Jason Cromwell standing on the boardwalk on the other side of the street. Next to him was a bigger man who resembled him, and both men were staring.

Slowly, Nathan released her, taking both hands in his.

"You'd better go inside. I'll send Timothy over later."

"Nathan, please be careful."

She suddenly stood on her tiptoes and reached up to press her velvet lips to his rough ones, sending a chill through him. He drew a deep breath as she backed away, but her kiss remained like fragrance on his lips.

Still holding her hands, he swallowed hard, then turned her

so that she couldn't see the Cromwells, and as she entered, he quickly closed the door behind her.

Then he pulled on his slicker and turned, but the Cromwells were gone. So the other one was Titus. Maybe they knew something about Wolf. It would be like them to hire a man like that.

As he crossed the street, he saw Timothy and Quincy coming out of the store. They were both laughing and biting at striped candy. Nathan grinned with pleasure, and the three of them went to the hotel.

But the Cromwells were at the saloon with the Corleys and Sheriff Eichner, and the surly young brothers were ready to kill Nathan.

"Not so fast," Jason said. "You got to do it so Titus and I are out of it."

"We got reason to gun him," Trapper Corley said, picking at his mustache.

The sheriff grunted. "Just make it fair. I'm gettin' a lot of pressure from the governor's office."

"We'll get him," Brick Corley said, rubbing his fat nose. He was the largest and meanest of the brothers. "In fact, I may just take him with my bare hands. That fair enough for you, Sheriff?"

"Who took a shot at Reed?" the lawman asked. Slack, the skinny one, grinned. "Maybe it was old man Beeler."

"It was Slack," Brick said, shifting his big frame. "I guess I ain't taught him good enough. He missed."

Trapper scratched his mustache and grinned. "Beeler would have missed the whole street."

But old man Beeler was busy climbing the back stairs of the

hotel in the rain and heading for the front balcony, a shotgun in his hands. The sheriff had told him about Nathan's room and what he looked like, and Beeler had seen Nathan at the open balcony door from down in the street.

He was a crusty old man with a wiry beard wet from tobacco juice, his face deeply lined, his stringy gray hair poking out from under his floppy hat. He wore an old wool coat, and he was shivering.

He moved under the roof overhang, carefully approaching the open glass door. He didn't want to hang for this, but nothing would do but Nathan Reed knew why he had to die.

He peered through the curtains that were softly blowing on either side of the glass door. The boy was curled up on the bed, chewing on some candy. A grubby looking man with a gray mustache was lounging in a chair. And Nathan Reed was in another chair, cleaning his six-gun.

Beeler jumped inside, shotgun aimed right at Nathan.

"Nobody move."

Timothy sat up, and Nathan motioned him to move over to the wall. The boy obeyed. Beeler was grim, his shotgun still pointed at Nathan as he moved away from the door.

"I figure you're Nathan Reed."

"You figure right."

"You killed my boy."

"You must be Mr. Beeler."

"That's right. And I come to send you to your maker."

"You'd kill an innocent man? The Lord wouldn't like that."

Beeler was waving his weapon. "Don't give me no fancy talk. You killed my boy."

"He was trying to knife me. Ask Chavez. He was there. We

were both asleep in the stable. Your son came in with a knife afore daylight."

"Jason said you went after my son."

"I figure he or Rachet put your boy on me. They're right scared I'm a government agent."

"Are you?"

"Maybe."

Nathan kept shoving the cleaning rod through the barrel of his Colt. He could see that the old man was hesitating.

Beeler looked at Quincy. "What about you?"

"That's Quincy. And my son."

"You take a shot at me earlier?" Nathan asked.

"I kill a man, I do it face to face. That was one of the Corleys."

"Ever killed anyone before?"

"Yeah, sure. I fought with General Lee."

"And this is what you come down to? Look at you. Dirty all over. You smell somethin' awful. And those clothes, they oughta be burned to kill the fleas."

Beeler straightened, his face wild with anger. "I oughta blast you right now."

Nathan peered down the barrel of his Colt. "No, Mr. Beeler, because you're not a killer. A rustler and chicken thief maybe, but outside the war, I figure you ain't never killed nobody."

"I ain't never took no chickens."

"And you ain't no killer."

"Try me."

"First you'd kill me, and maybe *Quincy* there, *if* he didn't get you first, but what about my son?"

Beeler was agitated, but his fury had been dispelled. He lowered his shotgun. "Blast you. I come here to revenge my son, and now look at me. And you ain't even got a spittoon in here."

He turned and spat out the window, then turned quickly, but no one had moved. "Ain't right," he said. "A man's got to revenge his son."

"Then get the man who put him on me."

"Jason?"

"No. Rachet maybe."

"That slime?" Beeler turned and spat again. "I hate his guts. All of 'em, always tryin' to cheat me. I bring 'em cattle, and they don't wanna pay nothin'."

"Your cattle?" Nathan asked.

Beeler had to grin. He sat down on a wooden chest, his shotgun across his knees. "If you're a government man, the answer is yeah, sure, they're my cattle. And if you're not, well, maybe they used to be Chisum's, but he don't miss nothin'. So what are you goin' to do about it?"

"I'm not after you," Nathan said.

"Yeah, good, well, I'm small potatoes, right?"

Timothy moved back to the middle of the bed, licking his candy. "Why don't we give him a bath, Pa?"

And to Beeler's surprise and violent protest, he ended up in a tub full of hot water with Quincy pouring clean water on him, Nathan looking on, while Timothy waited in the room.

Nathan took a chance and told Beeler about Wolf.

The old man bent down to wash his beard, then looked up. "Wolf, eh? Never heard of him, but I know about them markin's on those dead men. You want me to help find 'im? How much?"

"Fifty dollars if you spot him for me."

"For fifty dollars, I'll get him myself."

"No," Nathan said. "He'd kill you sure. He wasn't a Comanchero for nothin'."

"Well, I'm on the trail a lot. I'll keep my eyes open."

"And for ten dollars, you don't tell anyone."

"Mr. Reed, you and me are gonna get along just fine."

Nathan had to agree, and when Beeler left, he was a new man. Quincy had brought him new clothes and a slicker. He sat taller in the saddle as he rode out of town.

"You trust him?" Quincy asked.

Nathan grinned. "Yeah, darn'd if I don't."

That evening the rain stopped, and Nathan went to see Dooley, who was eating at the cafe. He told him it was one of the Corleys who had shot at him, but he had no proof except the ravings of an old man.

And this time, Nathan told Dooley about Wolf and asked for secrecy.

Dooley's face was filled with surprise. "Well, I'll help you if I can, Nathan."

"No tellin' who he is, so watch yourself."

"I can't figure who it might be. Sounds like some kind of animal. No one around here. Maybe he's just camped out in the hills like some varmint."

"Not with all that army gold."

"Been three years, Nathan. I figure that was melted down and spent a long time ago."

They left the cafe and went into the moonlight. Nathan felt he could trust this man, and he walked with him along the boardwalk as Dooley made his rounds.

They could see the lights in the boarding house, and Nathan thought of Leslie. He was glad she was away from the

Cromwells, but he was still worried about her.

At the same time, he was thinking of his wife, a woman he had loved since childhood, and she had died because he hadn't been there to protect her. His guilt and anguish had been directed into revenge, the only way he could handle it, but he knew that someday he would have to face it.

But first he had to find Wolf.

"Me and Quincy, we' re going huntin' tomorrow."

"Maybe I'll come along," Dooley said.

Suddenly, a shot rang out, whistling past Nathan's ear and singed Dooley's right shoulder, then slammed into a post.

SEVEN

*D*ooley spun with six-gun in hand, but Nathan had already drawn and was jerking Dooley against the wall of a store. The wounded deputy dropped to one knee.

"I saw the flash," Nathan said. "I'll get 'im."

"Wait—"

But Nathan was sprinting across the street toward the alley near the hotel. The rifle barked again, cutting the brim of his hat, but Nathan kept running, dodging, firing back. Again the rifle blasted, missing him.

He charged forward, into the alley, seeing a running figure in the darkness. Nathan kept dodging and following. The man turned and fired, then ran behind the hotel.

Nathan reached the corner and stopped.

He was breathing hard, sweat running down his neck. Suddenly, he darted out and rolled onto the ground, just as the rifle barked, and Nathan fired again.

The man leaped into the air, jerked and fell.

Nathan got to his feet, drawing back the hammer again, but the man was dead in the moonlight, sprawled out on his back, staring at the stars in the sky.

Dooley came running and poked around the comer, then joined him. Both men stood looking down at the skinny dead man.

"Slack Corley," said the deputy.

"I didn't figure he had the guts to face me head on."

"Well, Brick and Trapper Corley, they sure won't hold back. Maybe you'd better get out of town afore dawn. I got to get patched up."

"I ain't runnin'."

"You want to find this Wolf or not?"

Nathan hesitated. Dooley stepped back to peer down the alley. Men were coming out of curiosity.

"Go up the back steps," Dooley said. "I'll take care of this. You got your boy to think of."

"All right, but I'll be back."

Before daylight, Nathan and Quincy took Timothy over to the boarding house. The front door was open, and the boy paused in the light of the outside lamp.

"Pa, I oughta go with you."

"No, you stay with Leslie. She may need you."

"But I don't have a gun."

Nathan pulled out some greenbacks. "Quincy said you was admiring a small carbine over at the store. Even the way they been discountin' this money, this should be enough. You go ahead, son."

Timothy's round face brightened. "Wowie, thanks Pa."

Nathan reached down to hug him, then left with Quincy.

Riding through the mountains, they saw many signs, some Apache, others horses and cattle. They passed ranches with smoke curling from the chimney and saw men herding stock. Buzzards circled, and the land was muddy and wet, but the sun was warm in a gray sky. Nathan liked it better in the hills. He felt stifled in town.

"A man can breathe out here, Quincy."

"Men like us, we got to ride free, Nathan. That's why I ain't lookin' to marry. Of course, I did have a Cheyenne wife once, but she died a long time ago. Even that wasn't like stayin' put. They was always on the move."

Nathan shrugged. Yes, they loved the land and being on the trail. Scouting had been a way to get out here and ride, to feel the wind in his face and know the dust was rising behind him. That's why Nathan hadn't been home when he was needed. That was his deepest pain, and his need for the wanderlust had been shattered.

When they rode back into town that late afternoon, the two remaining Corley brothers were watching from in front of the general store. Trapper was hanging back with his Winchester under his arm. Brick was moving onto the boardwalk.

Brick was the biggest and strongest. He had big hands and a fat nose in the middle of his mean face. His shoulders were huge. He wasn't wearing a sidearm, but he looked deadly. Sunlight glinted on his greasy face.

"Hey, Reed."

Nathan reined up and leaned on the pommel. "Sorry about your brother, but he came after me."

"Yeah, that's what Dooley said."

Nathan straightened and lifted his reins, then stopped as Brick moved into the street, his face red with anger.

"But I'm gonna kill you with my bare hands."

There were men standing in the shade at various buildings, all watching and waiting. Some were grinning, anxious to see a fight, others were plenty nervous.

"I got no reason to fight you," Nathan said. "Get off, or I'll pull you down."

Slowly, Nathan wrapped his reins around the saddle horn, then stepped down from the black. He didn't unhook his Colt from its loop in the holster, nor did he remove his gunbelt. He didn't trust Trapper, who was still watching with the Winchester, although he knew Quincy would back him up.

"Out here in the mud?" Nathan asked.

"Well, now, are you afraid of getting a little dirty?"

"You like rollin' in the mud, you must be part pig."

Brick snarled. "Don't get smart with me, Reed. You don't wanna die the hard way."

Nathan hooked his Stetson on the saddle horn, then moved away from his horse, his hands at his side. He was calculating how hard it would be to escape that powerful grip that was about to reach for him. Brick weighed twice as much as Nathan and was muscle bound. He could break Nathan's back.

They stood in the muddy street in the sunlight, some ten feet apart. Men were gathering on the boardwalk. There were some women, but Nathan didn't know if Leslie was there. There was no sign of Timothy.

He did see the Cromwells standing in front of the hotel.

And Jose Chavez moving to stand near Trapper, his own Winchester ready in case the man tried to gun Nathan.

Brick was getting anxious, moving a little closer, his giant hands spread with fat fingers ready. His eyes were beady and narrowed, his mouth twisted. His boots were sucking mud as he moved, his body hunched up and ready to spring.

"Come on, Reed."

Nathan took cognizance of the surrounding area. In front of the boardwalk behind Brick was a wagon and team. There were no other horses at the railing, which rose on either side of a big wooden trough now filled with rain water. The rest of the street was clear.

Up on the boardwalk, at the general store where some of the men were standing, barrels of flour and other goods were sitting under the roof overhang, along with rolls of barbed wire and some pitchforks.

Down the street in either direction were more stores, some with their wares out in the sunlight. Men were gathering, anxious to see a fight.

Brick was snarling. "Come on."

Nathan felt sweat trickling down his back. If he got in those clutches, the man would break him in two. He began to circle slowly.

Brick bared his ugly teeth and rubbed his fat nose. He moved as Nathan moved, both circling and watching like roosters, each figuring their best move.

Suddenly, Brick charged like a grizzly. He grabbed for Nathan, who sidestepped and tripped him. Brick went crazily forward, slipping as his feet went out from under him. He landed on his belly.

Laughter rang out from some of the men watching. Furious, Brick scrambled to his feet, slipping and sliding until he was upright. His belly and front of him were covered with mud. Nathan backed toward the railing near the wagon. Brick was furious.

"Blast you, stay still."

Brick charged again. Nathan went to sidestep but lost his footing and slid right into the big man. Fat hands grabbed Nathan and wrapped him up like a sausage as they crashed into the railing, breaking the pole and rolling onto the boardwalk.

Getting to their feet, Nathan fighting to free himself from the man's iron grip, they swayed and struggled. Nathan pounded the big man's face and jaw to no avail.

Brick growled with pleasure, trying to break Nathan's back. Putting his feet against the railing post, Nathan pushed hard.

Brick stumbled backwards and sat down on the rolls of barbed wire. He screeched and let go, and Nathan, gasping for air, staggered free.

As Brick came up again, his muddy boots skidded and he lost his balance, turning to grab at the wall. But he fell facedown on the barrels, smashing two of them. He rolled over and got to his feet and stumbled around, holding his rear. His front was covered with mud, sugar and molasses.

With a roar, covered with brown slop, Brick charged again, but now he was really slippery, and Nathan slid right out of his grasp.

"Blast you!" Brick roared.

He charged again, and Nathan sidestepped. Brick stumbled and dropped to one knee, then grabbed for a pitchfork. Nathan slammed his fist down on the back of the man's neck, kicked him in the rear, and shoved him sideways into the watering trough.

Losing his balance, Brick fell like a rock, crashing on his side, then splashing about on his rear. Hot with anger, Brick got up and fought his way free of the trough. It was then his brother Trapper threw him the pitchfork.

Nathan seized the broken railing pole. It was handy, but only four feet long, while the fork had an eight-foot reach.

The two men were back in the muddy street, dancing around as best they could, boots sucking mud. Brick kept stabbing at Nathan with the fork. Nathan kept dodging, the pole in his hands, but he couldn't get past the steel prongs that were slashing closer and closer.

Suddenly, Brick charged like a wild man.

Nathan leaped aside, losing one boot in the mud.

As Brick came past, he slammed the pole into the man's middle. Brick's eyes went round as he gasped for air and staggered past, dropping the fork and doubling up, then falling to his knees in the mud, whining.

Nathan pulled his boot out of the mud and sat back on the boardwalk. He was breathing hard as he shoved his foot into the wet leather. He grabbed the post of the roof overhang and pulled himself to his feet, but he could barely stand. He had some of the mud and molasses on his new shirt, but he didn't care. He was just glad he was alive.

He turned to see Chavez with the barrel of his rifle stuck in Trapper Corley's side. Relieved, Nathan moved to sit on a barrel of flour. He was hurting all over.

Trapper went out to help his brother, and the two men staggered off in the mud toward the other side of the street. Brick was obviously in a lot of pain, and they headed toward the doctor's office.

Nathan looked up to see Quincy still on his horse, leaning on the pommel and grinning. The black stood near him, ears perked up and watching nervously.

Dooley came to stand by Nathan.

"I thought he was going to kill you."

Chavez came to kneel at his side. "Nathan, those brothers aren't goin' to give up, and now they will not be so careful. Better watch your back from now on."

Nathan saw Timothy running across the muddy street, slipping and falling and stumbling onto the boardwalk.

"Leslie wouldn't let me help, Pa."

"I'm all right, son."

He looked across the street to where she was standing with two other women. She was in the shade, but he could see she was smiling. Wearing a new blue dress and cape, she looked striking.

Timothy grabbed his arm and knelt by him. "I'm sure proud of you, Pa."

Nathan took his hand and stood up slowly, a bit unsteady, Chavez helping him. His whole body ached as he walked out into the muddy street, his son at his side.

"Quincy, would you mind takin' care of my horse?"

"What am I, your groom?"

But Quincy was grinning, and he reached for the black's reins and headed for the distant livery. Nathan grinned, then took his son across the street. Chavez and Dooley followed.

Leslie was standing alone now, and she looked relieved.

"Oh, Nathan, he could have killed you."

"He sure tried."

"Pa beat him, didn't you, Pa?"

"Timothy, you go with Leslie. I have to talk to Dooley and Chavez here."

"Aw, Pa."

"Señora," said Chavez, "I'm told you do not live at the Cromwells' now. I was thinking—"

"About Lupe? She's still there."

He blushed under his dirty beard and turned away with Nathan and Dooley.

Standing alone and watching from across the street, the Cromwells were concentrating on Leslie. When she saw them, she quickly turned away. Jason frowned, his searing eyes burning under his heavy brows.

"She's afraid of us," Titus said.

"No, it's you. Remember down in Mesilla? I saw you lustin' for her, and she musta known you was undressin' her with your eyes. You stay away from her. I'll call on her later."

"Why do you get first call?"

"I sent for her. I took her in. I bought those clothes."

"She needs a real man," Titus snapped.

"You?"

"She ain't been with a man yet. She needs me." Jason laughed. "Come on, Titus, you have no delicacy. I'm what she needs. Gentility."

"You can fool the whole town. And maybe you can fool Leslie, but I know you, Jason. So don't put on airs with me. When we were kids, it was you torturin' the chickens, not me."

"I know all about you, too, Titus. You're an animal. So back off."

"All right, let's forget it for now. But what are we going to do about Reed? Paine's gettin' nervous and could blow our whole operation."

"Well, we just have to make sure Reed has nothing to report. That is, until he's dead. I was hopin' old man Beeler would go after him. Maybe now Trapper will call him out."

"Yeah," Titus growled, "but Rachet says Reed is pretty fast.

He could beat Ole Trapper. Me, I got a better idea."

"Don't you be gettin' arrested."

"Not me. But over in Lincoln, there's a hard-case we can send for. A real fast gun. Trabajo. And he's for hire."

"I thought he was dead."

"No, but Reed soon will be."

EIGHT

That evening, Leslie was leaving the boarding house and walking down the street toward the cafe near the courthouse. Timothy was at her side, bouncing along and kicking rocks off the boardwalk. She was wearing her blue dress and cape.

"I'm so glad your father is having us for supper."

"Yeah, I'm real hungry."

She paused, for in the twilight's glow, she saw Jason and Titus across the street, and now Jason was crossing. He was wearing a fine new suit and long coat and looked like a senator, but he still had that strangeness in his eyes. He hurried onto the boardwalk while Timothy glared at him.

"Leslie, I'm so glad to see you."

"I'm meeting some friends for supper."

"Will you dine with me tomorrow night?"

"I don't think so, Jason. School starts next week, and I have to prepare. Besides, I will have Timothy with me."

Jason controlled himself. "Leslie, I do have to talk with you. You owe me that."

"Timothy, wait for me up the street."

The boy was grim, but he went on ahead.

"What is it, Jason?"

"Why did you move out like that? Not even a word."

"Jason, I needed to be on my own. I felt like I was going to be suffocated at your house."

"But I bought you clothes—"

"That bought you nothing, Jason," she said, fiercely.

"I didn't mean that. I meant I was trying to help you."

"All right."

"So won't you come back?"

"Not with Titus there. Besides, I have a job now."

"Are you afraid of Titus?"

"Yes."

"He won't come near you." Jason wiped his brow. "Leslie, don't you know? I've been in love with you since the first time we met."

"Jason, I'm grateful for your concern, but—"

"If Titus moved out, would you—"

"I'm staying at the boarding house, Jason."

"Look, I'm asking you to marry me."

She flushed with color and drew back a little. "Thank you, Jason, but I've only been widowed six months. Ask me in another six months, if you wish."

"I saw you kissing Nathan Reed."

"He's a friend."

"Then let me be your friend."

She stared at him a long moment, her face hot with rising anger. "Goodnight, Jason."

"Leslie, after all I've done for you."

"What have you done, Jason?"

He wiped his brow again. "I mean, I gave money to Paul for your wedding. When he was killed, I sent for you, and I took you in, and—"

She turned on her heel and headed up the street, heart pounding in her breast. Jason was a good catch financially and socially, but she was a little afraid of him, and she was terrified of Titus.

Still, she had no chance with Nathan, and she had met no one else as yet, although men were often following her about trying to carry things or help her across the street. Women had short lives on the frontier, so there would be many widowers. And the usual bachelors frantic for a cook and housekeeper with a ring on her finger.

Yet she was terrified that anyone who wanted to marry her could end up dead. Like Paul. No, she was foolish to even entertain the thought. A brother could not kill a brother. Still, Titus was not quite human.

She caught up with Timothy, who took her hand.

They went into the cafe where Quincy, Dooley and Nathan were waiting. Nathan had a clean shirt on, and he was sporting his new leather vest.

Timothy managed to have Leslie sit next to Nathan, and they ordered steaks for dinner. Over coffee, Timothy spoke up, still annoyed.

"Jason Cromwell was botherin' Miss Leslie."

"What did he want?" Nathan asked, turning.

"He wanted me to live in his house."

"And you turned him down."

She smiled. "Yes, but not because of Jason. Titus is still there."

"And if Titus moved out?"

"That's what Jason was suggesting when he asked me to marry him."

Nathan's mouth went dry. "And what did you say?"

"I said it was too soon."

Nathan relaxed and sipped his coffee. It tasted right good now, and he leaned back, glancing at her. She sure was lovely, but he had no right to even consider her. His wandering ways had already lost him a woman he loved. He couldn't do that to Leslie. Yet, being near her was the highlight of his day.

Dooley was arguing with Quincy. "Well, I say, Victorio's down in Mexico by now."

"Ain't much he can steal down there, and this is his home."

Dooley looked at Nathan. "You think Victorio's back?"

Nathan shrugged. "Maybe. Either way, all them Apaches headin' south will be joinin' him. The stronger he gets, the more likely he'll come back."

"Me and Nathan," Quincy said, "we're takin' another run through the hills tomorrow. Old man Beeler's gonna help us look."

"Beeler?" Dooley asked, surprised. "I thought he'd be gunnin' for you."

"We sort of worked things out," Nathan said. "The man's not a killer in the first place. And in the second place, he just needed a hot bath. Fleas can make a man awful surly."

Timothy laughed, while Dooley and Leslie stared.

Dooley shook his head. "Well, I might come along. There's a few questions I could ask that old man."

That night in the hotel, Timothy and Nathan sat up late while Quincy snored away. They were staring out the balcony door at the stars and moon.

"You think we'll ever walk on the moon, Pa?"

"Looks pretty small to me."

"Miss Leslie says someday there'll be men up there. I mean, she's been readin' all these books."

"Man can't fly. Ain't natural."

"Still, it's a nice idea, huh, Pa?"

"Yes, son."

"I sure like Miss Leslie, Pa. She's a real lady."

"She don't need the likes of us."

"But she really likes you, Pa."

"I was a restless man, Timothy, and Crook needed me, but I should have been home when the ranch was raided. I'm to blame, and it's eatin' me alive."

"No, Pa. There was about forty or fifty of 'em. They would have killed you, too. Nobody could *stop* 'em. If you'd been there, you'd be dead, and I'd be all by myself. I'm glad you're alive, Pa."

Nathan paused, looking down at him. "Thank you, son."

"They come over the hill like a stampede, Pa. I heard this sound, and I thought it was thunder. I looked out of the barn and—"

Timothy's voice broke, and he leaned against his father.

"It's all right, son. It's better forgotten."

"I keep tryin' to remember, Pa. If I could see their faces again, I could point him out to you."

"What do you mean?"

"I ain't no kid, Pa. I know you're here lookin' for Wolf. I heard some fellas talkin' about Chavez's men and how they was marked."

Nathan slid his arm around his son. "All right, Timothy, but keep it to yourself."

Tears filled Nathan's eyes, and he was glad for the darkness.

The next morning, Timothy went to the boarding house, and Nathan rode out of town with Quincy and Dooley, heading for Beeler's ranch. Quincy had his old Sharps along with him, claiming-the newfangled Winchesters had no range.

For the next few days, the trio joined with the old man and hunted for traces of Wolf. The killings had all shown tracks of six to seven horses, so Wolf was not alone, but he had not reformed his horde of killers. Dooley had a lot of questions for Beeler, but the old man never admitted rustling or any dealings with the Cromwells.

Until Dooley offered him ten dollars for information.

"I'll sure see what I can find out."

The men camped out in the hills, while Jason made more overtures to Leslie, even at the schoolhouse. Titus kept in the background. Rachet and Paine made several trips to town, and the Corleys impatiently waited for Nathan to return.

One morning in the hills, Nathan rode up onto a rise and surveyed the surrounding terrain. Green grass was everywhere. The sky was pure blue like a bird's egg, and the breeze was soft in the warm sun.

A bullet slammed into the top of his left shoulder, spinning him and his horse about. The shot echoed in the wind. He dug in his heels, and the animal scooted down the slope, then slid on the grass down to where Dooley, Beeler and Quincy had been riding.

Nathan was in pain, blood on his shirt, but it was more of a crease. It just hurt like blazes.

"Stay here," Dooley said. "We'll get 'im."

"No, I'm ridin' up this draw. Quincy, you head back around

the hill. Dooley, you and Beeler get up where you can see 'im, but don't show yourselves."

"But you're hurt," Dooley argued.

"Just a scratch."

Nathan shoved his bandanna inside his shirt, drew his Winchester from the scabbard, worked the lever to throw a shell in chamber, and headed up the draw on the nervous black. Quincy went the other way, and Dooley dismounted, climbing the hill on foot, Beeler at his heels.

Nathan was sweating, pain shooting through his flesh on the top of his shoulder, but he was angry. Back-shooters were lower than a snake's belly. Maybe it was the Corleys, or some of the Cromwells' men, but even better, maybe it was Wolf and his outfit.

Nathan moistened his dry lips, his Winchester heavy in his hands. He headed his horse up through the brush, then onto the rocks. It was too noisy, iron hooves slapping on stone, so he dismounted and left his horse behind. He moved on foot while hot blood oozed down inside his shirt.

As he got down and started to crawl, he felt sweat running down his rear. Moving up the grassy slope, he heard his heart pounding so loud he feared they would hear it. He drew a deep breath and continued to climb on his belly. As he reached the edge of the rise by a cottonwood, he saw them.

Three of them riding forward, all smiling.

Three ugly, bearded men with floppy sombreros and dark gleaming eyes. They rode stiff and straight in the saddle, but they were liquored up and enjoying themselves.

"I shot him out of the saddle," the lead rider was bragging.

"Wolf will pay us a lot of gold," another said.

Grim, his face burning, Nathan leaped to his feet, rifle aimed. "Up with your hands."

Nathan wanted them alive, but the men spun their horses and drew their weapons, firing even as Nathan jumped aside.

He pulled the trigger and hit one square in the chest. The others kept firing. Another bullet hit Nathan on the left arm, and he dropped to the ground, firing and missing.

Dooley, Quincy and Beeler came running, firing their weapons as the two remaining bandits whirled their horses, then charged them. Quincy dropped to the ground, took aim, and knocked one out of the saddle. Beeler got the other.

The shots echoed in the stillness of the hills.

There was a long silence that followed. Nathan dragged himself to his feet. Quincy came running, and the others followed. The three bandits were dead, and Dooley knelt to check them, Beeler joining him.

Quincy was more concerned about Nathan. "Well, at least they didn't get your gun arm. I swear, Nathan, I can't let you alone for a minute."

Nathan grinned as Quincy started tearing his shirt. "Ow, darn it. Be careful."

Quincy bared Nathan's arm and wrapped his bandanna around it. "At least your shoulder ain't bleedin' so bad."

"Look," Beeler said, standing up with a shiny object in his hand. "A gold watch. Chain and all." Nathan looked at Quincy, who hurried over to Beeler.

"Does it have a name on it?"

"Sure, but I can't read."

"I can. Roberto Sanchez."

Beeler grimaced. "Well, I shot him. I get the watch."

Quincy turned to Nathan, who was staggering over to them. "It's the watch, all right, Nathan. From Chavez's place."

"So we got three of 'em," Nathan said.

"Means Wolf's got three maybe four others around here."

"Look," Beeler said, suddenly.

Up on the skyline, there was a fourth bandit watching.

"He's out of range," Dooley said.

"No, he ain't," Quincy said with a grunt.

The old trapper laid his Sharps on Quincy's shoulder and took high aim. Then he drew a deep breath and pulled the trigger. The weapon went off like a cannon. The bandit was knocked clean out of the saddle, and his horse spun around.

Dooley and Quincy mounted and rode up to check the man, but he was dead. They tied him on the saddle and brought him back down.

It was then they saw the cavalry patrol heading their way. It was the black troop with the big sergeant in the lead, and Smith came over to them, then dismounted as Dooley filled him in with the story.

Smith frowned. "Well, I can't take them back to the fort without the watch."

Beeler began to whine. "But I ain't never had a gold watch before."

"I'll try to make sure you get it," Smith said, "but I got to prove these men were killers. It's the reason they're dead. You don't want charges against you."

"He's right," Dooley said.

Beeler reluctantly turned over the watch. "Only gold I ever had. Except for my teeth."

Smith turned to Dooley. "Unless you want 'em."

The deputy shook his head. "No, it's better this way."

The troop soon left with the dead men tied on their horses, and Nathan smiled.

"Well, he'll ride in a hero, but Paine will take the credit."

"And I ain't never gonna see that watch," Beeler said.

"Look," Nathan said, "you help me find Wolf, and you'll get a gold watch, chain and all."

"And my fifty dollars?"

"Yep."

"Then let's get crackin'."

But further search was fruitless. Nathan, Dooley and Quincy returned to town, confident that Beeler and his men were already out rustling cattle to sell to the Cromwells.

"I'd like to catch that old man," Dooley said, "but I got enough to worry about right now."

"Like stayin' alive," Nathan warned. "They're bound to get the idea you ain't to be reckoned with. And you sure ain't on their side."

At the little schoolhouse, twelve children were leaving, boys pulling pigtails, girls squealing, everyone laughing.

Timothy stayed behind to wipe the blackboard as Leslie looked at the slates she had collected. There were more than a dozen chairs at the benches, and on the walls, there were drawings the children had made. Timothy was whistling to himself.

Abruptly he turned. "Miss Leslie, why don't you marry my Pa?"

Startled, she drew back, her face flushed. "Well, Timothy, he hasn't asked me."

"Would you say yes?"

She was even redder. "Timothy, I don't know."

"Well, do you like him?"

"I admire and respect him."

"Then it's a start."

"But your father, he doesn't want to marry anyone."

"Why not?"

"Because he can't stay in one place."

"I know that, but Ma never minded so much."

"Well, Timothy, I'm afraid I would."

"So you don't wanna marry him?"

Her face was burning. "Timothy, it's out of the question."

"There's one way."

"And what's that?"

"You got to be like him. Both of us, we got to ride like him. We got to move all over the country. Like he does. You know, sleep under the stars. See what's over the next hill."

She stared at him, then shook her head. "No, Timothy."

He was disappointed. "Will you think about it?"

"Timothy, let your father live his life as he wishes. He's been through enough."

"Phooey."

She smiled, reaching to draw him to her. "But if it were ever possible, I'd think about it."

He grinned, hugged her, then headed for the door.

She followed, and as they stood on the steps in the fading sunlight, they saw the riders coming in from the hills.

"It's Pa, and Dooley, and ole Quincy."

Leslie breathed a sigh of relief. "Come, we'll go meet them."

Timothy grabbed her hand and hurried her down the slope toward the men as they hit the main road and reined up to wait.

As Timothy neared, he freed her hand and ran forward, grabbing his father's right leg.

"Pa, you're hurt."

Leslie felt a tightness in her middle. She hurried forward to take the reins of Nathan's horse, leading it into the street. Tears stung her eyes.

"Nathan, are you all right?"

"Just creased me in a couple places."

"He's a tough old bird," Quincy grunted.

Later at the doctor's, Timothy and Leslie paced in the front office while Nathan was being treated in the back. Leslie kept wringing her hands, and Timothy bit his lip.

Finally, the old doctor came out with a smile on his worn-out face. "He's fine. Bullet missed the bone."

Leslie breathed a sigh as Nathan came into the room, his left arm and shoulder bandaged. He was wearing a sling, and he looked tired.

"Hey, Pa, you okay?"

"Sure, son. I just need to rest up. You can look after me, unless you want to stay with Miss Leslie."

"Stay with a girl when I can be with you? You're funnin', Pa."

Leslie smiled. "Yes, he's funnin'."

"We been doin' great in school, Pa."

"Well," Leslie said, "I can see need for improvement."

Nathan grinned and put his hand on his son's shoulder, then paused to look at her. Just being around her made him feel at home, and her smile was just grand. "Maybe you'll have supper with us, Leslie. At the hotel."

She was hesitant, knowing the Cromwells could be there, but she nodded. "I'd love to, Nathan. If Timothy agrees."

"Sure."

They crossed the street, the mud now dry and caked, and went up the steps of the hotel. The ornate lobby had some well-dressed men and women wandering about, but the dining room was empty except for the Cromwells. Both Titus and Jason were in their fine suits, and the two men stood up quickly.

"Leslie," Jason said. "Please join us."

"No, thank you, Jason."

Jason shrugged. "And your friends, if you wish."

"No, thanks," Nathan said, "but I got some news for you, if you're interested. We killed four bandits in the hills. One of them had a gold watch taken from one of Chavez's men."

Titus looked meaner than ever. "So?"

Jason nodded. "What's that got to do with us?"

Nathan studied them, then led Leslie and his son to a corner table where they sat and enjoyed their supper.

Titus sat down with Jason, his mouth tight as he muttered under his breath. "I'd like to kill that man myself."

"He must have got four of our men."

"Just keep your voice down."

"I thought you sent for Trabajo."

"Yeah, but he ain't here yet."

"Just take it easy, Titus. That temper of yours will get us in trouble yet. We want Reed to be shot down in a fair fight. Leave us out of it."

Titus glared at his brother, then bent a table knife into an elbow shape with his bare hand.

And across the room, Nathan watched them, wondering what the two men were thinking and what they were saying. He was weary, and his wounds were painful. Yet sitting here with Leslie and his son was so pleasant, he didn't mind.

Later, they walked Leslie to the boarding house. At the steps, Timothy conveniently stayed behind, pretending to be kicking a rock down the slope.

She paused at the door, gazing at Nathan in the lamplight. She touched the sling, then adjusted it.

"You're a brave man, Nathan."

"Will you be all right?"

"Why do you ask?"

"I saw the way the Cromwells looked at you."

"Jason's trying to be a gentleman. I am afraid of Titus, but Jason won't let him bother me. So don't worry, Nathan."

"You need us, you holler."

"I will, Nathan. I just hope you find the man you're looking for. Maybe then you'll be at peace."

He moistened his lips, his throat dry. She was so lovely, so compassionate, her eyes glistening. How he wanted to hold her and find comfort in her embrace. Yet he turned to leave.

"Nathan."

He paused, slowly looking back as she moved toward him.

She slid into his open arms, startling him, and then he drew her tight against him, avoiding his bad shoulder but holding her warmth until it invaded him, giving him the comfort he sought.

Slowly, his arms fell away, and she drew back, gazing up at him. "I can't tell you what to do, Nathan, but you have a fine son. He would be lost without you."

"I know."

"This Wolf could kill you, Nathan."

"Leslie, I can't tum back."

"Then may God ride with you."

She put her hand on his right arm and stood on her tiptoes. He drew a deep breath as her soft lips touched his rough mouth, sending a fever running through him, leaving him shaken as she drew back.

She waved to Timothy, then went inside. Nathan took another deep breath and came down the steps, her kiss still burning his lips. He saw Timothy's smile and put his hand on the boy's shoulder.

"Let's turn in, son."

"She's a nice lady, Pa."

"I know, son, but don't get too attached. When our work is done, we'll be riding out. Unless you want to stay here and go to school."

"I want to be with you, Pa."

Nathan nodded with relief, and they headed for the hotel, but he saw a light in the sheriff's office and paused. If it was Dooley, he wanted to talk with him. If it was Eichner, he'd turn around and leave.

Inside, they found Dooley with his feet up on the sheriff's desk, grinning at them.

"I get comfortable when I'm alone."

"No one locked up?"

"Are you kiddin'? All the bad guys work for Cromwell. They never get locked up. I've done it, but they always get out, so what's the use?"

Nathan studied him. "What's got into you?"

Dooley sat up straight, turning grim. "I'm disgusted, that's what. Afore we headed out, I had one of Jason's men locked up for stabbin' a fellow down at the cantina. I come back, he was long gone. Let go. Vamoosed."

"Maybe you need a change of scenery."

Dooley nodded. "Could be I'll ride out with you when this is over. Head north. Or to California. Just keep movin'. That's best, ain't it?"

"Sometimes."

There was no use talking to Dooley this night. He was acting weird, so Nathan and Timothy left the office and headed across the street toward the hotel. There was no light in their room, but there was a movement outside the balcony door.

Nathan paused, reaching for his Colt.

But already there were shots, and the figure vanished into the shadows.

"My God," Nathan breathed. "He got Quincy."

NINE

*N*athan ran across the street. "You stay back, Timothy."

But the boy was on his heels. Nathan ran around behind the hotel, and Timothy went inside. Hurrying along the back wall in the darkness, Nathan was breathing hard and watching the stairs. He saw a figure. He fired as it darted back.

Now the figure was out of sight, probably running around the front balcony.

Nathan went charging up the stairs. He went around the wall but paused at the comer. Peering along the balcony, seeing nothing but posts and railing. There were a few chairs, but no sign of life. Some of the doors were open. The attacker could be in any one of them. Just waiting.

Nathan moved cautiously, his Colt ready.

He felt cold down to his boots, but sweat was trickling down the small of his back to his rear. His heart was thumping. Any moment he could be dead. He tried to swallow, but his mouth was too dry.

He could see that Dooley was standing in front of the sheriff's office across the street, looking around and trying to figure where the shots had come from, his rifle ready.

Nathan had no way to signal him.

Slowly, Nathan moved along the outside wall to the first doorway. He peered inside. The room was empty. He climbed in and went out to the hallway, moving down toward his room.

He prayed Timothy was down in the lobby.

The door to his room was open. Nathan kicked it further. He peered inside. Timothy was kneeling over Quincy, who lay on the floor by a bunk. Nathan muttered under his breath and headed toward the open balcony door.

Just then a figure darted into the balcony door, firing wildly at Nathan. Nathan shot twice. The man jerked and fell forward, rolling into the room and kicking, then abruptly sprawling lifeless.

Nathan came forward in the moonlight, bending down.

It was Trapper Corley.

Grim, he was about to turn when a shot rang out. Nathan spun, six-gun ready. But the big assailant was staggering forward from the hallway, grabbing his chest and gasping, then crashing facedown on the floor.

Rising with his small carbine smoking in his grasp, Timothy could only stare. But he had just saved his father's life.

Nathan rolled the man over with his boot. It was Brick Corley, a bullet square in the heart. Now the Corleys were all gone.

Quickly, Nathan went to the lamp and struck a match, bringing up the flame in the smoked glass, then turning to see Timothy moving toward him.

"Pa."

Nathan, still holding his six-gun, slid his good arm around his son. "You saved my life, Timothy."

The boy sobbed with the trauma. They heard footsteps in the hallway. Dooley came charging in with his rifle cocked. He paused, staring at the Corley brothers.

"Is Quincy all right?"

"I don't know," Timothy said, turning.

Nathan caught his breath, suddenly hopeful. He knelt with Dooley as they turned Quincy's face into the lamplight.

The old trapper opened his eyes, blinking at them.

"I think I got shot."

"Sure did," Dooley said. "Twice."

"Get the doc," Nathan said, and Timothy took off running.

Later in the doctor's office, Quincy was grumbling as the bullets were removed from his back and shoulder.

"Same place I got it a year ago."

Nathan was perched on a table, watching, shaking his head. Timothy was grinning with relief, and Dooley was busy telling everyone what to do.

"We don't have to worry about the Corleys now," Dooley said. "But it ain't finished. They'll get you yet, Nathan. Why stick around? You ain't never gonna find that Wolf."

As soon as he said it, Dooley went blank.

Nathan and Quincy looked at the boy.

Dooley made a face. "I'm right sorry, Nathan."

"It's okay," Timothy said. "I figured it out. Pa's here lookin' for Wolf. And I'm gonna help 'im."

Nathan went to put his hand on Timothy's shoulder. "Let's go outside, son."

In the moonlight, Nathan walked with his son to the center of the street and spoke softly.

"Listen to me, Timothy. When you saved my life, you became

a man. But you should know, I don't want you anywhere that Wolf can get his hands on you. It'd tear me apart."

Timothy leaned on his father. "I know, Pa, but I sure don't want anything to happen to Leslie."

"Why do you say that?"

"I don't know. Just a bad feelin'."

"Wolf never works a town. He may be here with some false identity, but he won't do anything in Black River. He works like a wolf, hunting in a pack, but out there, son. In the hills, where he can get away."

"I hope you're right, Pa."

They went back inside to swear the doctor to secrecy as to their hunt for Wolf.

"Don't worry about me," the old man said. "I been around longer than any of you. I'll still be here when you're gone, patchin' up the likes of you. Now let me get some sleep."

Back at the hotel, Quincy flopped wearily on his bunk. "I reckon it ain't safe to leave the blasted window open."

"It's a door," Nathan corrected. "But you're right. Just the same, now that we've gotta lock it, seems like you oughta get yourself a bath. Me and Timothy, we may get sick with no air in here but the smell of you."

Timothy laughed. "It's okay, Quincy. Mornin's soon enough."

"That's mighty kind of you."

"I guess you'll be laid up awhile," the boy added.

"Not me. I've walked around with bullets stuck in me for weeks, and I fought a lot of Kiowas while I was doin' it. You'll learn one thing, young fella. Me and your Pa, we don't stay down easy."

While the three of them settled down for the night, a stranger was riding into town on a black horse. His clothes were black, and so was his hat. He had silver on his hat band and fancy gunbelt, and there were conchos on his saddle. His boots were carved right fancy. He rode straight in the saddle, his hand on his thigh, looking around carefully.

He reined up at the livery and bedded down his horse.

Then he walked back to the mansion he had spotted when he had come in from the east. He swaggered up to the light of the lamp on the front porch, then paused to roll a smoke and light it, pressing it between his thin lips.

His face was thin and hard. There was a twist to his narrow nose, and his jaw was crooked. Meanness glowed in his near white, gray little eyes as he knocked on the door.

After a long while, Lupe opened it. She was in a dressing gown, and she stared at him.

"Mr. Cromwell's expecting me."

Nervous, she made him wait. After a time, Jason came downstairs with his smoking jacket over his nightshirt and let him inside. Titus also came down the steps, but he was still dressed.

In Jason's office, the three men had whiskey.

"You shouldn't have come here," Jason said. "You were supposed to meet us at the saloon."

"The town's asleep, and no one tells me what to do."

"We're payin' you mighty well," Titus reminded him.

"You want me to kill somebody named Nathan Reed. Well, I never heard of him."

"He's mostly been an army scout," Jason said, "but our man at the fort says he's a mighty fast draw."

"He kill anybody?"

Jason nodded. "The Corley brothers. The Beeler boy. And some of our men."

"Corleys? They were nothing."

"And a lot of Apaches, Jason added.

"Listen to me, Trabajo, "*Titus said,* "we don't care how you do it, but get rid of this man."

"In my own time, yes."

"We want it done right away," Jason said.

"Listen, my friends. I am still alive because I am very careful. I will see my prey. I will talk with him. I will know him."

"And then?" Jason demanded.

"And then I will kill him. In a fair fight."

"We don't care how," Titus said with a grunt.

"But I do. I have a reputation. No one will pay big money for a back shooter. But for a fair fight and a dead man, they will pay anything. Like you did."

"All right," Jason snapped. "Get on with it. But don't come here again. Now here's the thousand up front. You get the rest when he's dead."

Trabajo smiled, his swarthy face showing satisfaction, and he left with the money. When they heard the front door close, Titus slammed his big fist on the desk.

"Maybe we'll just get rid of him when this is over."

"We may need him again."

"I tell you, Jason, I'm tired of this place. I don't like wearin' these fancy suits and puttin' on airs."

"But I need you to help with the business."

"As soon as Reed is dead, I'm leavin'. And I'm takin' Leslie with me."

Jason leaned back with a sneer. "No, Titus. She's not going anywhere with you."

"You forget who I am."

"And you forget who I am, little brother."

They glared at each other a long moment.

Then Titus grunted. "Well, let's see how it goes with Trabajo. I'm beginnin' to think nothin' can kill Nathan Reed. I may have to do it myself."

"We got other things to deal with. Like Beeler. I got word he's helping the law. He was even there when they got those four men of ours. Get rid of him."

"Who's givin' orders around here?"

"He's deliverin' cattle to Little Creek Canyon tomorrow night, Titus. Get there and kill 'im."

"I'll have it done, but stop tellin' me what to do." As the two men snarled at each other, Lupe crouched on the staircase, her ears burning with what she had heard. She slipped back upstairs. Just after midnight when all were asleep, she was dressed and climbing down the backstairs and running down the street, breathless and frightened.

It would never do for an aristocratic lady to go to a man's hotel room, so she kept running up the street and headed for the boarding house. On the steps, she dropped to her knees, frantic and fighting for air. She didn't want to be seen. She didn't trust the mayor or his wife, who ran the boarding house.

Abruptly, she went around behind the building and tossed pebbles at Leslie's glass *window* that served as a door to the balcony. Soon the curtains parted. The door opened, and Leslie came out to peer down, startled to find Lupe climbing the big barren tree.

Leslie leaned on the railing and whispered.

"Lupe, I'll come down."

But the woman was up on the first *limb*, leaning close to tell her about Trabajo. Leslie was startled and shaken.

"This man, where is he now?"

"He went to the hotel."

"We must warn Nathan."

"I do not think he will do anything now. He is like a cat with a mouse."

"You get back home, Lupe. I'll tell Nathan first thing."

"And tell him Mr. Beeler' s going to be killed at Little Creek Canyon tomorrow night when he delivers some cattle. And maybe he ought to send for Señor Chavez."

Lupe slid back down the tree, scraping her hands and muffling her cry, then heading off in the darkness.

Leslie began to wash her face. It would soon be dawn, and it was Saturday. There would be no school.

Dressed in her riding skirt and heavy jacket, she slipped out of the boarding house and down the steps to the front door. Outside, it was very cold and damp. A pale glow of red lined the eastern horizon where the mountains met the valley.

Her boots clicking on the boardwalk, she hurried with her breath short. Jason would never approve of her going to a man's hotel room. She frowned at the thought.

Crossing over the dry mud of the empty street, she rushed into the empty hotel lobby. The elderly clerk was asleep at the desk, his head rolled onto his arm. She went up the stairs as quietly as she could.

Knocking softly on the door she knew was Nathan's, she glanced up and down the hallway where lanterns glowed, worried she would be seen.

"Nathan," she whispered.

The door opened, and a hand took hers, pulling her inside. "Leslie, what is it?"

Timothy was turning up the lamp. Quincy rolled onto his right shoulder on his bunk, his left arm in a sling just like Nathan's. They were all fully clothed, except Quincy who had his shirt off. They all looked at Leslie in surprise.

Nathan led her to a chair, and she sat down to catch her breath, then told them about Trabajo and Beeler.

"Trabajo," Timothy said. "That means trouble in Spanish."

"It means sidewinder," Quincy snarled. "I heard about him. He's fast, Nathan. And he ain't never backed down to anyone. I hear he likes a big audience."

"I'm not worried about him right now," Nathan said. "We got to get to Beeler. Keep him alive."

Quincy sat up. "We'd better get Dooley to go with us."

"I'll get him," Timothy said.

"And take Miss Leslie home," Nathan added.

Taking her hand, he pulled her to her feet, but she resisted, backing away. "I'm going with you. I can shoot."

"Me, too," Timothy said. "You're both staying here."

She was unhappy. "Nathan, I have to do something."

"Then keep an eye on what goes on around here."

"I could see Jason. He might tell me things."

"You stay away from him."

"We're wastin' time," Quincy said, getting to his feet.

Leslie put her hand on Nathan's arm. "There could be a hundred men in that canyon. Lupe thinks you should send for Mr. Chavez to help."

"We need more than him," Nathan said. "We need the army. Those black soldiers. Except for Oakley, I can't trust anyone else Paine's got."

"I'll get 'em," Timothy said.

"I'll go with him," Leslie said.

"It's a two-hour ride. You could run into Apaches."

"Not on the main trail," she argued.

Nathan frowned. "You know better than that. Get Lupe to send some of her Mexican friends instead. They can take care of themselves. You can't."

Leslie squeezed his arm. "Be careful."

"It's okay," Timothy said. "You can kiss 'im."

Before Nathan could react, she rose on her tiptoes and kissed his weathered cheek. "Go with God."

Soon they were parting in the silent, empty street as first light cast long luminous shadows. The men picked up Dooley. Leslie and Timothy had to figure a way to get to Lupe, and it was midmorning before Leslie lost her patience.

They walked to the mansion and pounded on the door.

Lupe answered with surprise, then quickly came outside.

Leslie took her hand and led her down the sixty-foot walk to the street, Timothy following.

"Lupe, Nathan wants the black soldiers to come to Little Creek Canyon before dark. Can you send someone?"

"Si, I have friends. At the cantina."

"Then let's hurry."

Lupe glanced nervously back at the mansion. "Señor Cromwell will be looking for me, but I will go."

"I lived most of my life in Texas. I speak Spanish. Tell me who to send."

It was then Jason Cromwell appeared on the front steps, calling to them. Lupe whispered frantically, "See Ricardo at the cantina."

Jason come swaying down the path, his face red. He was in his smoking jacket and looking very annoyed. His burning eyes were fixed on his housekeeper.

"Lupe, where's my breakfast?"

"Right now, Señor. Señora Cromwell was asking me to go riding with her."

"That's absurd, Leslie. There are Apaches and rustlers out there."

Leslie tried to appear surprised and perplexed. "I was just getting restless, Jason."

"Come and eat with me."

"No, I had breakfast."

"Will you have supper with me?"

"No, I'm sorry. Timothy and I have plans."

"Then let me call on you. Say two o'clock?"

Leslie hesitated. Despite Nathan's warning, she felt she would be safe at the boarding house. "All right."

"Good."

Leslie turned and went back down the street along the boardwalk, Timothy at her side. Only Jason's mansion and the little cantina were at this end of town.

They would soon be passing the cantina, but she was afraid to look over her shoulder until she was almost there. She paused, casually turning. There was no sign of Jason.

They hurried through the broken swinging doors of the little cantina. Chairs were upside down on the tables. There was no one there. She called out frantically.

"Ricardo?"

A woman came from the back room. She was small with her gray hair in a bun, and she seemed angry until Leslie began to speak hurriedly in her broken Spanish.

The woman disappeared, and Leslie drew a deep breath.

She turned slowly and walked out into the sunlight, Timothy taking her hand.

Standing on the boardwalk was Jason Cromwell.

TEN

Nathan led the way through the canyons in the deep hills north of town. Scattered pines and brush dotted the grassy slopes. The sun was high in the sky, and it was plenty warm.

Dooley and Quincy followed. The trapper still had his arm in a sling, but he was acting as if he had never been shot, his old body ignoring the pain. Their horses picked their way over rocks and dried mud.

"We oughta be there by nightfall," Dooley said.

Quincy grunted. "Let's hope the army gets there in time."

"I wonder how many we'll catch," Dooley added.

Nathan was silent, thinking about Beeler. He liked the old man. He didn't particularly want him in jail, but he didn't want him dead either. Beeler had been helping them track Wolf, so a judge might be lenient. If one ever was willing to come back to Black River.

It was nearly dark when Dooley pointed out the entrance to Little Creek Canyon. They were on a rise in a circle of aspens, resting their horses. They stood quiet, looking in all directions. After awhile, Dooley spoke.

"I figure the herd will be coming in from the north, at the other end, if they was raidin' Chisum again."

"This Chisum must have a lot of cattle," Quincy grunted.

"He's a choice target," Dooley said. "His herd is so big, he has trouble keeping 'em all in."

"And the Cromwell outfit will be comin' from town," Quincy added. "Unless he has men camped out here somewhere."

Dooley frowned. "There are a lot of places to hide. The hills and canyons are very steep. But the cattle have to come out this way or he'll never get 'em to the reservation agent."

Nathan rode down to the trail by the creek and found the tracks of some twenty men, heading into the canyon. He rode back up to where the others waited, telling them what he had learned. The Cromwells' men were already waiting for Beeler.

The others mounted and rode to a vantage point high above the canyon. Daylight was fading slowly. Nathan turned to Dooley and Quincy.

"You stay here and try to keep 'em boxed in the canyon. I'm goin' around the back to try to pull Beeler out of this."

"I'm goin' with you," Quincy said.

"No, you stay with Dooley."

Night was falling fast as Nathan rode along the ridge, trying to keep out of sight. The canyon was deep and narrow, the walls mostly red sandstone. A little creek ran through it, the water silvery in the twilight.

Now he saw the camp of twenty men. Their horses were saddled, but the men were having coffee and relaxing. He was too high up to recognize any of them, but none was big enough to be a Cromwell. The herd was not there. But further up, he saw the dust.

Nathan kept going through the trees and rocks, hoping he could get to Beeler in time. When he found a deer trail going down the steep wall, he hesitated. He didn't know this black horse that well, but he had to take a chance.

He started down, the animal skidding through the rocks, Nathan leaning way back with loose rein. The black kept going, down, down, down, plummeting toward the canyon floor that was still some hundred feet below. One slip, and it would be the end of Nathan.

He felt the dryness of his mouth and throat, the beating of his heart. The black kept sliding and fighting the terrain, and now it was catching itself here and there, slowing them down, making its way step by step, dust all around them, and then they were on the canyon floor.

The black stumbled up to the creek and stopped, shaking.

Nathan reached down and stroked its damp neck.

"Thanks, friend."

He straightened, seeing the lead steer working its way toward them. He backed his horse to the wall of the narrow canyon and let the herd work its lazy way past in the clear light of the full moon.

More than a hundred head of cattle moved by, their brands having been altered with running irons. Some had been botched, but a reservation agent could easily look the other way.

Four men appeared, and one of them was Beeler.

The other three were young and nervous.

Beeler was startled to see Nathan, and he sent the young riders on ahead with the cattle.

"It's a trap," Nathan said. "The Cromwells want to kill you."

"What about my hands?"

"He don't care about them. He found out you was helpin' us track Wolf."

"What's that to them?"

"Maybe they think you can't be trusted. If you're helpin' the law on Wolf, you might spill somethin' else. Now let your boys go on with the herd. The army's on its way."

"Hah. Paine won't do nothin'."

"That black troop might. They ain't been around long enough for Paine to get to 'em."

"Paine's from the south. He'd never bother." Beeler worked his lined face and wiry beard. "So now what?"

"Dooley and Quincy are up ahead. They'll try to keep 'em in the canyon."

"Well, I don't know how you got down that wall, but I don't figure we can get back up. So now what?"

"We could stampede your cattle."

Beeler snickered. "Good idea. Let's get the boys out of here and send 'em home."

The young hands, already nervous, willingly turned and headed back for Beeler's spread. Nathan and Beeler moved up behind the herd. Over a hundred head could make short work of the camp a half mile up the narrow canyon.

They waited until they were a little closer, then pulled their Winchesters. The herd was already uneasy with the dark, unfamiliar passage, some spilling on both sides of the creek.

Nathan and Beeler started yelling and firing into the air. The startled cattle threw up their heads. Long horns rattled. And they were off at full speed, raising dust and a roar like thunder.

The herd charged around the comer and right into the camp where men were trying to mount. Some were climbing the walls and falling back down. The frightened cattle ran over several men, knocked two horses and riders down, and kept going with the other riders in front trying to outrun them.

As they neared the opening to the canyon, rifle fire broke from the ridge. The riders tried to rein up and fire back but could not, with one horse stumbling and throwing its rider under the herd.

Twelve men were left, and they turned toward the south wall of the canyon, trying to reach the trees for cover. Two reined up on the slope to fire back, and both were shot out of the saddle. The other ten thought they would make it to cover, but Quincy had moved to the other side and was firing in front of them. They fired back, and he got two.

Within minutes, the black troop was riding up the creek toward them from the south. The surviving eight men threw up their hands and let their horses move back down to the trail.

Sergeant Smith put his men in command of the prisoners then rode to Nathan and Beeler. Quincy and Dooley were working their way down the slopes.

Smith leaned on the pommel of his saddle, studying Nathan. "I ain't quite figured you out. Are you workin' for the government or not?"

"No," Dooley said. "I am. I was sent here by Washington to work undercover."

Everyone stared at the young deputy.

Nathan grinned. "Well, I trusted the right man, all right."

"And I'm trusting all of you," Dooley said. "As far as Nathan Reed goes, Sergeant, he's after Wolf."

"The Comanchero? I thought he was dead."

"He's in these hills," Dooley said. "The four bandits we killed.

They worked for him. But my job is to get the Cromwells. About now, the auditor and special marshals ought to be at the fort. I figured it was the only way we were going to get them pinned down. There has to be a second set of books out there."

Smith sat quiet as he listened to Nathan and Dooley fill him in, then turned in the saddle to look at Beeler. "What about him?"

"He's workin' for us," Dooley said. "But the rest of 'em, they're likely on the Cromwells' payroll. What we got to do is prove it. I figure the books will do it."

The prisoners refused to say who hired them, so the soldiers took them and the cattle, leaving Nathan with Quincy, Dooley and Beeler. It was too late to go back to town, so the four men camped deeper in the hills.

"What I told you about my background is true," Dooley said, "but my uncle works for Indian Affairs. So they hired me to come out here and get some evidence on the Cromwells. I was hittin' a dead end until you came along, Nathan. You sure do stir things up."

"Well, I'm right glad you're here, Dooley. I was gettin' mighty fed up with the Cromwells' way of doin' business, but my mind was on Wolf. Now I know you're lookin' out for the government, I can rest easier."

Back in town at the Cromwell mansion, Paine was arguing with the Cromwell brothers. Rachet was sitting with his arms folded, his thin face solemn. Paine was red and angry.

"You let me down, Jason. You were supposed to change those agency books. Now how am I goin' to explain those extra five hundred Apaches? That fool agent isn't any help, you know. There's an auditor at the fort right now. Straight from the President. And he's got ten special marshals with him."

"Didn't you know he was comin'?" Titus growled.

"How was I supposed to know? And Rachet here, he ain't helpin' one bit with his fancy numbers. How am I gonna explain the difference in bids?"

Rachet scowled. "You control your soldiers, don't you?"

"What are you saying? Treason? I'd never get away with it, and you know it. That auditor can't be touched."

"So what's the answer?" Jason asked.

"Paine has to handle it," Rachet snapped. "He's got the second set of books in his safe."

Paine drew himself up. "They got everything that's in my safe right now, and I told you before, and I'll tell you again. I ain't goin' down alone."

"Then get out," Jason said. "Take what you got and run."

The officer worked his square face and bit on his cigar. "And what are you gonna do? The Cromwell Trading Company is finished."

"We got more cattle movin' to the reservation," Titus said. "They'll be there by mornin'. With good pay."

"Forget it," Paine said. "By mornin', I'll be arrested, and we'll all be headin' for prison."

"Then get out," Jason repeated. "Don't even go back to the fort. You neither, Rachet."

"What are you goin' to do?" Paine asked.

"This house is full of treasures. I hate leaving them behind, but I can start over somewhere else. I'll get wagons and ship some of it. They won't get to me that fast."

"You're fooling yourself," Paine said. "They'll be here at sunup, and you can count on it."

"Why?"

Paine's face was redder, darker. "Well, I made sure I wasn't going down alone. I mean I had to protect myself, so that second set of books, well, they show everything."

Jason reached in his desk drawer, pulled a pistol and shot Paine square between the eyes. The officer stared at him, mouth wide open, blood spilling. He dropped to his knees, then fell on his face.

Rachet was snarling like an animal. "I oughta skin him alive. Only it's too late. Now what?"

Titus rose like a bear from the stuffed chair. "We'd better move out. We got plenty of money and some of that gold left. Rachet, you get over to the livery."

"What about Nathan Reed?" Jason asked. "He'll be on our trail."

"Rachet, you stop by the hotel first, give Trabajo this extra bag of gold. Tell him to be out there in the mornin' when Reed shows his face. Get him right off."

"And the sheriff?" Rachet asked.

"We don't need him," Jason said. "Pay 'im well, but leave him behind."

"What about the deputy?"

"That kid? He's nothing. Don't even worry about him. We're headin' for Mexico."

"You're forgettin' somethin'," Titus said. "You framed Victorio for killin' some soldier boy one of your men shot down in the hills. That made Victorio awful mad, and he's out there somewhere."

"I'm not worried about a dirty Apache. You and me, we've handled a lot worse than Victorio."

Titus grinned. "Yeah, but the Comanches wanted somethin' in return. All Victorio wants is you."

While the Cromwells and Rachet disposed of Paine's body and then made their plans late that night, Timothy was in Leslie's room at the boarding house, pacing, his pink round face twisted. He looked out the balcony door at the bright moonlight as it caressed the big tree. He spun and paced some more, then played with the barrel of his carbine.

"You know ole Jason didn't believe us. He must have heard what you was sayin'."

"But he let us go."

"He scares me."

She was sitting at the dressing table, combing her long raven hair. Still in her riding outfit, she was weary and sleepy, but she was just as worried as Timothy.

"I sure wish Pa would get back."

"Lupe's friends said it was a long way. They must have camped in the hills."

"I'm worried about her, Miss Leslie. She ain't even come down to the store like she always does. Maybe we oughta get Mr. Chavez here."

"But how?"

"Same way we got the army."

"Good idea. Let's go."

"No, it ain't safe out there at night for a lady. I'll go to the cantina."

"Do you speak Spanish?"

The boy flushed. "No, but I can sure go at it in Comanche. A little Spanish though."

"Well, I'm going with you."

Timothy took his small carbine and Leslie pulled on her blue cape over her riding jacket and skirt. She was worried about Nathan, and the more she worried, the more she realized how she felt.

Paul had been a nice man, saving her from loneliness.

But Nathan was different. His very touch made her feel warm and loving. Being around him made her feel safe and wonderful, and he was a hero in her eyes. Yet she knew that what she had told Timothy was true. A wandering man should never marry. Still, that didn't solve her longing for Nathan Reed's embrace.

They walked out onto the porch, feeling the fresh cold of the night. Timothy walked with his carbine balanced, and she was proud of him. At the cantina, he went inside and brought out the small woman who took the message to find Chavez.

Leslie squeezed the woman's arm and turned to Timothy. "She will send for Chavez. And they will try to find others."

"I sure hope so, 'cause I'm worried."

The little woman hurried back inside the cantina. They could hear her chattering to someone inside.

Then, alone in the moonlight, Leslie and the boy turned to go back to the boarding house.

Suddenly, they felt big hands over their mouths.

ELEVEN

*A*fter camping in the hills, Quincy and Nathan rode into town, Quincy having removed the bothersome sling. Nathan had long since discarded his and had healed. Beeler rode along with them, figuring the Cromwells would be too busy getting out of town to bother with him. Dooley had gone to the fort to see the auditor.

Black River looked unusually quiet that early dawn, and Nathan felt a cold shiver down his spine. Quincy and Beeler were half asleep in the saddle, but Nathan was wide awake and alert.

As they entered the main street, they saw a man standing on the boardwalk in front of the entrance to the hotel. He was wearing black and silver, his pale eyes gleaming in the early light under the brim of his hat. A smoke dangled from his thin lips.

"Oh, oh," Beeler muttered.

"You know him?"

"Saw him once. Trabajo. Hired gun."

They reined up at the hitching rail, Nathan watching the

grim man with the crooked jaw. As they dismounted, they heard running feet on the boardwalk. It was a small woman, out of breath, a shawl over her head and shoulders.

"Señor Reed," she shouted.

When she saw Trabajo, she stopped and moved against the wall of the hotel, then backed to a store, then suddenly drew herself up, walked right past Trabajo and over to where Nathan and his friends were moving to the boardwalk.

"Señor Reed, they are all gone."

"Who's gone?"

"The Cromwells and that Señor Rachet. They killed Captain Paine. And they took Señora Leslie and your son. And they took Lupe. I sent for Señor Chavez, but it is too late."

Nathan felt ice water in his veins. He couldn't breathe. He felt nauseated. Leslie in the hands of the Cromwells, and Timothy, who would be of no value to them except as hostage against Nathan. His skin was crawling as his thoughts churned. Then he spoke to the woman.

"When Deputy Dooley comes to town, you tell him. He can be trusted. He's at the fort right now. Send word if he doesn't come in by tonight."

Trabajo walked away from the wall and into the street.

"Nathan Reed."

Slowly, Nathan turned to look at the killer. He knew the type, but he had avoided them until now.

"That man," the woman said, "he's paid to stop you."

Quincy was worried. "Don't do it, Nathan."

"I don't want it in the back."

Early light spread in the street. The eastern horizon was red and cold. The night chill lingered. Across the street, Sheriff

Eichner moved into the doorway of the jail to have a good look. Other men appeared, and there were faces at windows. The town knew what was happening.

Nathan's lips were dry and parched. His stomach was hurting bad. He had to save Leslie and his son, and this man was in the way. He moved slowly into the street, away from the horses. He needed an edge, and he didn't have one. He moved far enough so that if the sun rose, it would not be in his eyes.

Trabajo smiled. His eyes were like little lights in his swarthy face. His hand was dangling near his revolver. He figured he was going to make a lot of money in a few short seconds. This Reed person would not add much to his reputation, but the pay was unusually high.

Nathan stood with his hand at his side. Sweat trickled down his nose and rear. The only way out of town was through a paid killer. Nathan was fast, but this man was a professional.

"You first, Mr. Reed."

"You want this fight, you go for it."

"My, you are touchy."

"Either get out of town or make your move."

"Mr. Reed, you are a very anxious man."

Nathan swallowed hard. Time was of the essence. But he was not going to draw first. Not with Eichner and all those other men watching. Nothing must get in his way.

Trabajo twitched his cigarette up and down in his teeth. "Maybe the sheriff would call it."

Slowly, Eichner straightened and smiled, his fat belly moving with a deep silent chuckle. He came onto the boardwalk, pulling a large silver coin from his vest pocket.

Trabajo sneered. "When the coin hits the ground, Mr. Reed,

you had better draw, because I'm going to kill you at that moment."

Eichner was enjoying this. He flipped the coin in his palm a few times. Then he threw it high in the air between them.

Nathan caught his breath. All eyes were on the silver coin as it flipped in the early sunlight, then began to come down. It seemed slow, hesitant, coasting down like a leaf toward the crusted mud of the street.

When it hit, dust flew.

Trabajo's hand leaped to his holster, but Nathan's hand was equally fast. As both men whipped up their weapons and fired, Nathan danced aside, then hit the ground and rolled.

Having missed, Trabajo shot at the rolling figure, but Nathan had hit him on the side of his neck, and now, firing again, he hit the gunman square in the chest. Trabajo was surprised as he stood dying, his pale eyes crazed with the realization someone else was faster. His cigarette dangled from his lips, and he fell facedown on the dry mud, sprawling and lifeless.

Nathan got to his knees. He realized then his shirt was soaked with sweat. Dribbles ran down his face. His left shoulder where he had been wounded was hurting again. He was breathing hard and still shaken.

Quincy had moved onto the street with his Sharps. Beeler had his carbine balanced in his hands. The men watching backed away. Eichner retrieved his silver coin, then moved to the boardwalk, rubbing his fat chin. After a long moment, he yawned, then leaned on his office wall.

The show was over.

Nathan staggered to his feet and looked around. Then he holstered his six-gun. Trabajo lay silent in the street, ready for the human vultures to strip the silver, maybe steal his weapon for a souvenir.

"Come on, Nathan," Quincy said. "We got to get outfitted."

Nathan nodded. "Maybe we can pick up Chavez on the way. The Cromwells are bound to be headin' south to Mexico."

Quincy lowered his Winchester. "I reckon Wolf has to wait."

"Maybe not," Nathan said. "Not from what you told me about Rachet. And he's in with the Cromwells. They all came here after Wolf disappeared, remember?"

"Nah," Beeler said. "Them Cromwells is gentlemen. But maybe Wolf is one of their gang, all right. They got some forty men you know, aside from the ones we got up there. Every one of 'em ready to slit your throat for two bits."

"You comin'?" Nathan asked him.

Beeler worked his mouth. "Yeah, maybe I'll earn that fifty dollars you promised."

While Nathan and his friends got their gear and spare horses together, the Cromwells were moving south with a group of thirty-five men, along with Rachet who was acting as a sort of foreman. Their prisoners rode on one of the four wagons.

The two brothers were in the lead, both wearing trail clothes. Jason had a big knife at his belt. Both were heavily armed. Titus was wearing a new white Stetson that Jason had bought him as a gift. Jason was wearing a new black one for a change.

Titus twisted in the saddle. "Why'd you keep the boy alive, anyhow? He's just baggage."

"You got more faith in Trabajo than I have," Jason countered. "Nathan Reed's been indestructible so far. The boy will make a good hostage."

"We already got the girl."

"We're not laying a finger on her, Titus. And no one cares about old Lupe. We brought her along to tend to Leslie. But the boy? He means nothing to us. We'll need him if Reed shows."

Titus grunted. "Well, maybe you're right. But when we get through Apache country, we got to talk."

"About what?"

"You know what. The woman."

Jason smiled. "Trust me, Titus, she doesn't want you."

And that night, the Cromwells camped with a blazing fire in a canyon, convinced their numbers were too great to worry about the Apache, and they assumed the army would be a long time coming. The only one who might dog their trail so fast would be Nathan Reed, if he was alive.

After a hot supper, the prisoners kept to themselves, huddled in their blankets as the Cromwells cast glances at them.

"I thought Jason was a gentleman," Leslie murmured.

Lupe shook her head. "Señora, many gentlemen are thieves."

Timothy was very anxious as Leslie put her arm around him. "What is it, Timothy?"

"He's here."

"Who?"

"Wolf. I don't know who he is, but he's here. I feel it, Leslie. And I'm scared."

She hugged him. "Don't let them know."

"I feel like it's happening all over again."

"Don't worry," Leslie whispered. "Your father will bring help."

"But Lupe said that Trabajo was after Pa."

"Now, Timothy," she said softly, "we've both seen your father in action. Nothing is going to stop him from finding you."

"I sure wish I had my carbine back."

The prisoners gazed toward the ugly faces of the hired outlaws hovering around the fire and gear. They all seemed to have blazing black eyes and big hands. Rachet was moving about, his thin body like a pencil against the firelight.

Across the fire, the Cromwell brothers were busy settling down themselves. Titus leaned back and spoke in a low voice.

"Listen to me, Jason, you don't deserve that woman. I do."

"You can have a dozen women when we cross into Texas."

"We'll see."

"But until we settle this, you keep your hands off her."

Titus snarled but kept his voice down. "She gets to know us, she's gonna pick me. After all, I made her a free woman. And before any man got his hands on her."

"You what?"

"Sure, what good was Paul anyhow? He never did ride with us. He was ashamed to be around us, remember? What right did he have to shun me? He was a good for nothin'. He even turned me in to the army a few days afore he got married, but I got away. I hated his guts for that."

"What?" Jason muttered. "You killed our little brother?"

"Not me. I had it done. And that's why she's mine."

Jason reached for Titus' throat with both hands. Titus grabbed Jason's fat wrists and struggled. They rolled like sacks of grain, fighting for control, crashing against a rock, then rolling back across the grass.

Rachet and their men watched with greedy eyes.

Leslie sat up, frightened. Timothy looked around at the other men, then at the struggling brothers.

"Ain't nothin'," Timothy said. "Neither one can fight a lick."

Rachet went to break the brothers apart, and the big men got up, swearing at each other.

"Listen," Rachet said, "we'll never get to Mexico like this. What's got into you?"

Jason was so furious, his voice roared.

"He had my brother killed, just to get a woman."

Titus laughed, a sinister glee crossing his face. "You didn't really believe me, did you, Jason?"

"Yes, I believe you, Jason shouted. "You had Paul killed, and I'm not letting you put one finger on that woman."

"What'll you do, use your knife?"

Titus, stroking his short black beard, was smiling as he turned to look at the frightened prisoners. Leslie was staring at him in dismay.

"Jason's lying," Titus said.

But everyone watching knew that Jason was telling the truth. The surly men went back to their cards and conversation, but Rachet was already mentally counting the money he'd have if one of the brothers was gone. Still, he wanted to get to Mexico.

"Jason, you can kill him later. Right now, we got to get out of Apache country. Alive."

"We'll get out. I have a lot of friends down south."

"A long way from here," Rachet cautioned.

Titus was breathing hard, but Jason was puffing.

"All right," Titus said. "A truce."

Jason snarled and turned away, but he was already calculating how he could use this to get Leslie. He went over to where she was and knelt.

"I'm sorry, Leslie. I didn't know."

"Please, Jason. Let us go."

"Go where? You'd die out here."

Timothy was staring at Jason's long knife, sheathed at his belt. Lupe was holding Leslie against her.

"No one's going to hurt you," Jason told them. "Just get a good night's sleep. Tomorrow we have to go through Blanco Canyon. If we get over to the other side without running into Apaches, we'll make it all the way."

He left them, and Leslie turned to Timothy. "What's wrong?"

"I don't know. Things keep coming back."

She held him close. "For me, too, Timothy, but we've got to hold on until your father comes."

The three huddled together, and Jason went back to where Titus was talking with Rachet. He glared at Titus, but deep inside, Jason had wanted Leslie bad enough to want Paul dead. To him, she was sunshine and grace and endless beauty, a glorious warm and loving woman. He had to have her. She was everything he was not.

He lay back on his blankets, staring at the stars, and he rested his hand on his long knife. As soon as they reached Mexico, things were going to change.

TWELVE

Nathan reined up on the flats and twisted in the saddle.

The treeless grassland dotted with sage and some yucca spread in all directions. Back to the northwest were the snow-crested mountains near Black River. To their left was the trail west to the Rio Grande where they had found Leslie. And to the south was the way to Blanco Canyon.

Nathan, Beeler, Quincy and Chavez were alone on this trek, not having had time to gather Chavez's friends, for they had met him on the trail as he headed for town. They were well armed, and they had pack horses, but tracks confirmed the Cromwells had three wagons and some forty men.

"We're crazy," Beeler said with a grunt.

"You can go back," Nathan said.

"Not me."

Chavez wiped his mouth, his pot belly rising. "If they harm Lupe, I will kill them all."

Quincy leaned on the pommel of his saddle. "I'll lay ten to one that Victorio's hanging out at Blanco Canyon, and the Cromwell wagons have to go through there."

"They have a lot of men," Beeler said.

Nathan shrugged. "They ain't got enough men to stop me. They got my son. And the women."

They rode onward, each praying silently. They were facing terrible odds. The land was so open here, the Mescaleros or Cromwells could be watching from those cliffs to the south.

"We're only a few hours behind 'em now," Quincy said. "Army will never get here in time."

They passed the remains of a burned out ranch house that had never been rebuilt, the owners too terrified to return. They were far east of the stage road, and the way south was getting more dangerous by the minute.

But more so for the Cromwells.

Scouts returned from the canyon to advise Jason and Titus that the way was clear. The wagons began to move.

The white sandstone walls of the canyon rose hundreds of feet above them. The path was all sand and brush, following a dry creek bed. It was silent and empty.

"Take us an hour to get through," Titus said.

Jason let his brother ride ahead as a bigger target. But Jason was sweating. It had been his idea to frame Victorio for the murder of that soldier in the hills. After all, it was easy to believe. Jason's men had done the killing, but with Paine's help, the army picked right up on Victorio. After all, the warrior chief had done a lot of killing on his excursions from the reservation.

Titus had not given it a thought when Jason had bought him that new white Stetson. From the canyon walls, he'd sure look like Jason, who had always worn white hats until now. Not that Jason really wanted his brother dead. Jason just didn't want to die if Titus could take his place. Jason smiled and pulled his black hat down tight.

Moving into the canyon, the caravan hurried, but the wagons were heavily loaded with goods. The remaining army gold was in one of them.

As they reached the center of the canyon, all the men were sweating. Leslie, sitting on the wagon with Lupe and Timothy, stared nervously at the high walls.

Abruptly, terror broke loose.

Arrows whistled down. Bullets slammed into men and horses. There was no time to waste. The men on horseback broke into gallops, knocking Rachet and the Cromwells aside as they raced toward the far end, but more were knocked from the saddle. Some screeched and yelled as they were hit.

The driver of the prisoners' wagon leaped onto a riderless horse, leaving the wagon in a frantic craze. Timothy jumped onto the wagon seat and retrieved the reins.

Jason twisted in the saddle, desperate to save Leslie, but terrified for his life. He turned to see Titus rise up from his saddle with a screech. An arrow was right through his neck, and he clawed at it, then twisted and fell.

Timothy set the team into a fast trot, then whipped them into a gallop. Jason rode along side. Men were falling everywhere. The wagon wheels rolled over the bodies. Horses jumped over them.

Bullets spun by Jason's head. He set his horse to a gallop, then reined up, desperate for Leslie. He rode back, reaching for her, but she refused to leave the others.

"Blast you," Jason said, spinning his horse.

Arrows thudded into the wagon. One of the team horses

went down. Timothy leaped off and grabbed a riderless horse, then another. The women scrambled off the wagon and mounted. Timothy sprang up behind Leslie, and they were off. Only one wagon got through, the one with the gold, because they had three men on that wagon, and one was still alive.

As they left the canyon in a whirl of white dust, only Jason, Rachet, the prisoners, two half-breeds and a man called Blue survived. One breed was driving the wagon, the other leading the way. They crossed the open land, heading toward the protection of the distant hills.

It would be awhile before the Apaches could get down from their perch, and Jason wasn't worried.

"My friend Marcos has a ranch and a lot of men," he shouted. "It's like a fortress. Let's ride."

It was three hours later when Nathan and his party reached the entrance to Blanco Canyon. Buzzards were circling. They gazed up the walls, then rode near the looted wagons. Dead men and horses were all over. The bodies had been looted, some brutally knifed.

There was no sign of the prisoners.

As they neared the last wagon, they heard a sound. It was more than a whisper, a strange, gurgling gasp. Nathan reined up, Winchester leveled on the pommel, waiting.

"Over there," Quincy said.

Half covered with sand was the near-lifeless hulk of Titus Cromwell. An arrow was stuck down his throat, but he had managed to bury himself before the Apaches had come down from the walls.

Nathan knelt by him, but the man was slowly dying.

Titus' round eyes were filled with dismay that Nathan was alive. He reached a trembling hand to grip Nathan's vest.

"Don't let him have her."

"Who?"

"Jason. He's crazy. Crazy in the head."

"How do you mean?"

"He goes crazy. Uses his knife."

"Carves a 'W' on his victims?"

Titus nodded, his parched mouth fighting to get the words out. "Likes to torture."

Nathan wasn't convinced. "Sure it ain't you instead?"

"It's him. Don't let him cut her."

"You're sayin' he's Wolf?"

Titus nodded again, gasping for air. "Yeah."

"He's educated—"

"That's how he gets away with it."

"You know you're dyin'."

"Yeah."

"And you swear on your dying breath your brother was Wolf?"

"I swear."

"But why are you telling me now?"

"To save her. To save the woman."

"But the prisoners are unharmed?"

Titus nodded jerkily. "Yeah."

Quincy knelt. "We can't wait, Nathan."

"Don't leave me. You got time. They're goin' to Marcos' ranch. Big black butte. Like a fort."

Titus was coughing up blood. Nathan was torn between compassion for a human being and the trail that was growing cold.

"You want me to save her," Nathan said. "We can't wait."

Titus tried desperately to talk. He gripped Nathan's vest so tight, he nearly tore it from him. He fought to rise up, and then he fell back, eyes round in sudden death.

There was no time to bury him or the others.

"So Jason is Wolf," Quincy said, shaking his head. "It's mighty hard to believe. You think Titus was lyin'?"

"No. Let's ride."

Beeler was nervous. "What about the Apache?"

Chavez had been looking around. "I think they headed straight south. The Cromwells went southwest."

"Why didn't they foller 'em?" Beeler asked.

"They know the army's comin'," Nathan said.

"How do they know?"

"They always know."

They swung into the saddle and headed southwest. The Apaches left no further signs. The one wagon left deep ruts in the dirt and sand, and the tracks of six saddle horses raced ahead of it.

Nathan felt sweat covering his body. The killer of his wife and ranch-hands was within reach, but Wolf had his son and the women. He prayed they would be in time.

At the Marcos ranch, the Cromwell party reined up outside the open gate. The walls of the small fort had no sentries. As they entered, the group could see the picked bones of the dead. The house and barns had been looted.

"We can't stay here," Rachet said, frantic.

Jason was grim. "Fill up with water."

The well was pure. The Apaches needed water and were no fools. After watering the horses, the group filled their canteens and the barrels on the wagon.

The prisoners sat in the shade, watching.

"I'd like to get my hands on one of their guns," Timothy said.

Leslie slid something hard against his hand from the pocket under her cape. "I took it from the saddlebag," she whispered. "A pistol. But I'd better keep it for now."

"Won't be enough," Timothy murmured.

Lupe looked around carefully. "We have to try to get more. Right now our only hope is you, Señora, because he loves you."

They fell silent as Jason came walking over to them.

"We can't stay here."

Leslie allowed him to take her hand and pull her to her feet. She was so tired she could barely stand, and it was hot. He was pleased that she let him lead her to her horse.

"You won't be sorry, Leslie. I promise."

"I'm afraid."

"Sure. Me, too. But if we're lucky, the Apaches had some place else to go."

She stopped, and he paused. She gazed up at him with a need for tears but none came. "Jason, did Titus really have Paul killed?"

"My brother was an animal. A little crazy."

"And you think he—"

"I know he did it, Leslie."

"Then why didn't he come after me?"

"The army was after him. Paul had turned him in. Titus was a Comanchero."

"And you, Jason?"

"A businessman, Leslie. That's all."

He led her to her horse and helped her mount, then stood looking up at her. He squeezed her hand, smiled, and walked away. Leslie was nauseated, but she knew she had to keep her wits about her. Lupe was right. Jason was their only hope.

But Jason wasn't through with his plans. He turned to his men. "We can't take the wagon. Load the team horses."

Rachet stood around giving orders. When the other three men saw the small bars of gold bullion, they began to send furtive glances back and forth between each other. Jason didn't miss their intentions.

"Never mind," he said. "Any man puts a hand on my gold, he's dead."

"Says U.S. Army on it," Blue remarked. He was a hard-case with several scars on his face. "Maybe you oughta share it."

"Blue, just get it loaded."

But Blue turned his back, loading the horse but slipping a bar inside his vest pocket. When he turned around, the bar went right through, hit his gunbelt, and landed on his boot, then slid off into the dirt.

Jason was livid, eyes wild. He went crazy and pulled his long gleaming knife from its sheath.

Blue was terrified and jerked at his six-gun, stumbling backwards. Jason was on him with the knife. From Jason's throat came a weird, penetrating screech like an animal. He shoved the knife up through the man's chest into his heart. The man was dead on his feet, but as he fell, Jason was on his with a squeal, kneeling on his chest, cutting a crazed Won the man's forehead, blood spilling everywhere.

Leslie muffled her scream with her hands. Lupe looked away. Timothy stared and remembered, and he tried to get to the pistol in Leslie's cape, but she hugged him, stopping him and holding him so tight he couldn't move. But tears filled the eyes of the three prisoners, even as Lupe carefully moved her skirts over the dead man's pistol and kicked it over with her foot to press against Leslie.

And Jason mutilated the body. When he stood up, the big W on the man's forehead was the only readable mark. Breathing hard, huffing and staggering, Jason stumbled over to the well and dropped to his knees by the water bucket.

Leslie looked at the other three men, who were frozen in their tracks. The two half-breeds looked at each other and turned to their work. Only Rachet seemed undisturbed by Jason's being out of control.

Rachet came over to the prisoners. He wiped the sweat from his thin face.

"Ladies, don't say a thing to him. He won't remember much of it. He never does."

"What can we do?" Leslie whispered.

"Don't do anything, lady."

"Can't you stop him?"

"Look, lady, I ain't the one that's crazy. They don't call him Wolf for nothin'. He grew up that way. Half man, half animal."

Leslie shook her head. "And I was so sure it was Titus."

"Titus was a bad one, all right, but he wasn't hidin' it. What you saw of Titus, that was him. It's Jason you got to worry about."

Timothy was frantic, his memory back. He wanted to kill Wolf then and there, and it was all Leslie could do to restrain him.

When Jason rose from the well, his hands were washed, his knife clean and back in the sheath. He turned, stretched and rubbed his chin.

"I'm right hungry, but we can't stop here."

"We'd better move fast," said Rachet.

Jason didn't seem to see the dead man, he was looking for the pistol, and knowing they were in trouble, the prisoners moved away, leaving it there on the ground. Jason picked it up and shoved it in his belt.

"We'll make better time now. You men lead the pack horses and double up on one. You, Rachet, get Mrs. Cromwell's horse over here."

Leslie allowed him to assist her in mounting. She fought desperately not to recoil from his touch, holding her breath to control her fright.

"Just hang on, Leslie. It won't be long."

"Where are we going, Jason?"

"Mexico. I got friends to help us get there."

He turned away, and she knew he was talking about the Comanches, and she knew they had to escape long before that. But she didn't know how. And she had to control Timothy. If Jason went crazy, they'd all be dead.

THIRTEEN

*N*athan led his party to the Marcos ranch where it was set against the foothills. When he saw the dead man with the Won his forehead, he nearly went crazy himself. He was shaking and sweating, cold and hot. The man who killed his wife could kill again.

"We've got to get there, Quincy."

"Nathan, I know what you're thinkin', but we can't kill the horses, or we won't get there at all."

Beeler looked around at the carnage. "I tell you, I wish I was back rustlin' cattle about now."

"Workin' for the government," Quincy corrected him.

"Yeah, workin' for the government. Any place but here."

Chavez knelt outside the fort, looking around, and as they mounted, he spoke quickly. "The Apaches' signs are old. It's as we thought, Señor. They headed straight for Mexico from the canyon. They know the army is coming."

"Let's pray you're right," Nathan said. "But if Jason's headed into Texas where I think he's goin', we got more to worry about."

"Yeah," Quincy said, "Comanches."

They mounted and rode through the hills. They were worried plenty. And if they had to deal with Comanches, the best horsemen on the plains, they would be in real trouble. The warriors would take a real fancy to a woman like Leslie, and they would try to turn Timothy into one of their own.

Three hours ahead of them, Jason rode at a more leisurely pace, convinced the Mescaleros were not following them into Texas. He believed he still had friends among the Comanche. They had needed him, and as a white man, he could still obtain goods and weapons they could not.

Leslie was so worried, she was ill. Yet she tried to keep her terror out of her face. She worried about the furious Timothy who knew his mother's killer was riding ahead of them. Leslie kept the pistol under her cape, afraid to give it to him.

Rachet and the two half-breeds rode behind the prisoners. It would not be easy to escape. Lupe could not move as fast as Leslie or Timothy. They had no way of knowing that Nathan was alive or that any help was coming. If they escaped, they would be on their own.

That night they camped in a narrow wooded canyon at the base of some high ridges. They took a chance on a small fire. Huddled by the warmth with Lupe and Timothy, Leslie watched Jason making great promises to his men.

"Listen," she whispered to Lupe and Timothy. "If any one of you gets a chance to escape, do it. Don't look back. Just go."

"Give me the gun," Timothy whispered. "If I can get out of here, I can work from the outside. Ambush."

Leslie squeezed his hand. "If you get a chance, take it, but right now it's safer inside my cape."

Lupe hugged herself in the chill. "I would like to see that skinny little Señor Chavez about now."

"Careful," Timothy said.

They glanced toward Jason, who was leaving his men and strolling to the fire to light his pipe. He stood puffing it and showing off his body in the glow of the flames. There was no sign he knew what he had done with his knife.

Now he was strolling toward them. His eyes again had a life of their own, and now the prisoners knew why.

Jason smiled at Leslie. "See that ridge? From there you can see Texas. Come on, I'll show you."

"Jason, I am so tired. And that has to be a mile."

"No, come on, please."

She hesitated, but she knew she dare not argue with him. At the same time, if he should put his hands on her, he might feel the pistol.

When she stood up, she turned her back to him and let the pistol slide into the blankets. Timothy quickly covered it, his eyes big and round.

"Don't go," he pleaded.

"Don't worry," Jason said. "This lady is going to be my wife. I'll do her no harm. I promise you."

Jason had their horses saddled, and they rode up the slope toward the distant rise, fighting their way through the woods in the moonlight.

Rachet had wandered off with his rifle.

Timothy turned to glare at the two half-breeds.

"Why don't you give us guns? Take the gold and go, but leave us your rifles."

One of the half-breeds spat tobacco and muttered something.

The other just shook his head, then came to kneel near them. He had a hard, square face with many scars.

"You want to stay alive, you don't cross Jason. He would hunt us down like varmints. I have seen him do it."

"But he's going to kill us."

"Maybe."

"If I run away, will you stop me?" Timothy asked.

"Rachet will."

Timothy frantically looked up towards the rise where Jason and Leslie were outlined against the night sky. The moon was full, and the chill was as cold as the snow on the distant mountains.

Standing on the rim of the cliff, Leslie looked down at the terrible drop, straight down. Hundreds of feet below was Texas soil. Sandstone slides lay below them. Anyone who tried to get down here was heading for certain death.

She had an urge to push Jason off the edge, but she knew she couldn't budge him even if she caught him by surprise. Her thoughts startled her, and she knew she could not do it. She glanced back down the way they had come, at the tiny gleam of the fire. She could see men moving about.

"Look at it, Leslie. That's Texas out there."

"I know, Jason."

"That's right. You grew up in Texas. We have a lot in common."

"Jason, please let us go."

"Leslie, we're going to be married."

"Then Lupe—"

"You need a woman to look after you."

"Then let Timothy go."

"Not until I know that Nathan Reed is dead. Now as I was saying, see that tiny dark spot over there, way out? That's Sage Brush Flats. We can get horses there and supplies. Take us two days to get around these cliffs though."

While they talked, Leslie near faint with fear, the camp behind them, down in the draw, was quiet.

The small fire was surrounded by rocks, and Lupe was warming her hands. Timothy knelt near her, keeping the blankets close as he glanced at the men some twenty feet away. He whispered.

"Lupe, I got to do something."

"You do not know if the pistol even fires."

Timothy sat back, grim and angry at his helpless state.

Then he saw something. A movement, over in the trees, where the brush was clumped. It was either Apaches or someone here to rescue them. He prayed it was his father. He sat back, sliding the pistol under the blanket, then lifting the blanket around him, the pistol cold in his grip.

"Don't move, Lupe," he whispered, drawing back the hammer.

She grew tense. "What can I do?"

"Pour us some coffee."

She obeyed but was numb. Timothy stood up with the blankets around him. If it was the Apaches, they'd all soon be dead, no matter what they did. But if it was help, he had to warn them about Jason.

"Hey, boy," Rachet said. "Sit down."

"I got cramps in my legs."

Timothy walked about, stomping his feet.

Suddenly, men sprang from the brush. Quincy landed on

one half-breed, Chavez on another. Beeler tackled Rachet. They went sprawling.

Timothy pulled his pistol and ran around, wanting to help, yet looking for his father. He saw a figure that looked like Nathan riding up the slope, and he leaped bareback on one of the horses and took off after him, then slowed, trying hard to be silent. If anyone fired a shot now, Jason would take off with Leslie.

Quincy rolled with the half-breed, a knife slashing by his ear. He felt the man's brutal muscles, the power of a man born to the land. Quincy had a sore shoulder, and it hurt like sin, but he slammed his fist in the man's face, and they fought furiously for control.

Beeler shoved his pistol in Rachet's gut as they struggled but the weapon jammed. The man's knife slashed Beeler's ear. Rachet jerked backwards from his grasp, then Beeler jumped on him. They rolled, and Beeler shoved the knife up Rachet's belly, clear to his throat. Rachet died instantly.

Chavez was smaller than the half-breed he was fighting. The man's fingers clawed at his face. A knife flashed, and Chavez grabbed the man's fingers. They struggled, fighting and kicking. As the knife was suddenly twisted about and shoved brutally in the half-breed's chest, an iron pan crashed down on the dying man's head.

Chavez fell back, surprised to see Lupe standing there with the pan. "You could have hit me."

"Maybe I tried," she snapped.

Then abruptly, she threw her arms around Chavez and hugged him. He was so startled, it was a moment before he hugged her back.

Quincy suddenly jammed his knife into the half breed, and the man broke free, jerked, and collapsed in a heap.

The two half-breeds and Rachet were dead.

Now there was just Jason and Nathan out there, with Timothy on their heels. It was a long way to the ridge. No shots had been fired, so Jason had no warning.

Up on the rise, Jason turned Leslie into his arms.

"It won't be long. Now I want that for which I have waited so long, Leslie."

He drew her tight and bent his head to kiss her. Her hand suddenly was pressed against the knife scabbard. Before she could stop herself, she was pulling it free. Her act terrified her, yet the knife was in her hand as she tried to break away.

That act was nearly her death, for he became furious, shoving her back with a snarl as he seized the knife from her grasp. She fell down in the grass.

"Nobody takes my knife."

She lay staring up at him, but she was so beautiful, and he wanted her so bad, he gasped, trying to stop himself. His hand was shaking, the blade gleaming in the starlight. Any moment he could leap on her with slashing blade.

But he choked on his breath, and then he slammed the knife back into the sheath. He wiped his face with his handkerchief and turned his back. His big body was trembling. Then he coughed.

She was frantic, glancing down at the horses some twenty feet below and the distant campfire where people were moving around, unaware she could be dead in a moment.

But Jason drew himself up, wiped his face again, and turned around.

"Leslie, did you fall? Please, get up."

Too terrified to resist, she let him bend over and take his hand, but her mind was working furiously. She could take a sliding chance down that grade, but it would leave no need for Lupe or Timothy to be alive.

Jason pulled her back into his arms. His touch sent wretched horror creeping through her. Any moment he was going to kiss her. His heavy eyebrows and wide mouth were suddenly repulsive. Those strange gleaming eyes were fixed on her.

Out of the darkness, there was movement from the rocks, and Nathan reared up like a grizzly. He aimed his Winchester at the man.

"Let her go."

Jason held Leslie tight against him. "Put that down, Reed, or I'll throw her over the cliff."

Nathan hesitated as Jason sneered.

"No, Nathan," she pleaded. "He's the man you want. He's Wolf."

Jason's sagging face began to twist. "Listen to me, Reed, one more time. If you don't drop that rifle, I'm throwing her over the cliff."

"And you'll be dead."

Nathan didn't back off, the rifle still pointed at Jason's side. Leslie was gasping for air as Jason crushed her against him. She knew the cliff was certain death.

Abruptly, Jason pulled his knife and turned Leslie in his arms so the blade was at her throat.

"Now, back off, or she dies right here."

Nathan was grim but relentless. "You even scratch her, I'm blowin' your brains out."

Jason was getting frustrated. He didn't want to die. And he wanted Leslie too much to kill her. He suddenly threw her at Nathan. She fell into the rifle, and Nathan had to thrust her aside. But Jason leaped upon him. The rifle went off, firing into the air, then was lost in the struggle.

The big man's body was heavy, forcing Nathan to roll down the slope and crash into the brush near the startled horses. Nathan's sore shoulder screamed in pain. Jason's knife was slashing at Nathan's throat, but Nathan's hands were strong, gripping the big wrists and forcing the blade back and up.

Then Nathan brought his knee up into Jason's middle, shoving hard. Jason went rolling against a tree. Nathan rose up, pulling his six-gun, then losing his balance and sliding down the hill. Jason leaped on him again. The six-gun went flying.

Jason was an animal, squealing and clawing.

Nathan fought the man's weight, shoving him aside again and again. This time the knife was slashing Nathan's clothes, scraping his skin. He grabbed the big wrists and threw the man upward. Suddenly, Nathan had control of Jason's knife.

Seeing the blade in Nathan's hands made Jason growl. He rushed Nathan, who leaped aside and shoved the blade right into Jason's gut. Jason squealed, gasped, grabbing the knife handle.

Jason cried out like some wounded animal as he jerked the knife from his own gut and turned to go at Nathan.

It was then that two shots rang out. One from a rifle, the other from some pistol behind Nathan.

The bullets slammed into Jason's neck and the side of his head. He was suspended in midair for a moment, then went crashing down through the brush until he lay dead against some rocks.

Nathan looked up to see Leslie with his rifle. He thought suddenly of when she had shoved the stake into an Apache's back to save his life. He was amazed by her.

Nathan caught his breath and turned to see Timothy climbing the slope with smoking pistol. He grabbed his father, hugging him.

Quincy and Beeler were riding up to join them.

Nathan sat down, exhausted. "Where's Chavez?"

"Busy with Lupe," Beeler said. "She's already tellin' him what to do."

Nathan was still fighting for air. He sat on the cold ground and grasped for reality. It was here. The man who had murdered his wife was dead. Timothy was safe. It was over. And Nathan suddenly realized he was tired of more than this struggle. He was worn out, and he had lost his yearning for the trail. He wanted to hang his hat somewhere, for good.

Chavez came riding up with Lupe behind him.

Nathan turned and looked down at the far canyon where the tiny campfire was aglow. It seemed like a beacon. Timothy touched the blood on Nathan's arm as Quincy wrapped it with a bandanna.

"Pa, Jason was Wolf. I remembered. He was crazy."

"He was like two people, Timothy. He was a sick man."

Somehow that knowledge made father and son more at peace with the horror of the raid on their ranch.

Nathan held his son as he turned and looked up at Leslie. She was in a heap, hugging herself from shock. Quincy went to take her hand and help her down to where Nathan and Timothy were waiting.

She was trembling, barely able to move.

"Nathan, how did you know he wouldn't kill me?"

"He was in love with you."

She hesitated, wishing it was Nathan and not the dead man who was in love with her, not knowing that as he stared at her, he felt love trying to break free from the anguish he had been harboring.

"Nathan, your son was so brave."

"So were you," he said.

"Pa, Jason has army gold down in those packs."

"We'll take it back, son."

Beeler was complaining as usual. "Cold as blazes out here."

"Let's get going," Quincy said. "Those shots could bring a few unwanted visitors. We'd better move out."

"Too late," Nathan said.

Far below in the canyon, they could see the movements of many men around the campfire in the little canyon. Mescalero Apaches. About twenty of them.

Leslie put her hand over her mouth to muffle her cry.

"Pa, these women can't take much more."

"I know, son."

Nathan climbed to the ridge but kept low and close to the rocks. It was certain death to go down there, yet it might be their only hope. He looked to the right. No luck. To the left was a descending ledge four to five feet wide. He moved around the comer to look it over. It went most of the way down but could give way beneath them at any point.

"Let's give it a try," Nathan said.

"So much for the horses," Quincy grunted.

The group moved low along the ridge, avoiding the skyline, and they came to where Nathan had pointed.

Beeler coughed quietly. "We'll be killed dead."

"It's our best chance to stay alive," Nathan said. "The last twenty feet, we may have to jump."

"If we can get down, so can the Apache," Quincy said.

"They'd have to want us awful bad," Nathan argued. "Besides, they got Jason's goods and army gold. Victorio will feel vindicated. Come on. Chavez, you take Lupe. Lean back against the cliff as you move. I'll take Leslie. Timothy, you stay with Quincy."

"Yeah," Beeler said. "Who's gonna help me?"

Nathan went first, Winchester slung across his shoulder, Leslie behind him. They were pressed to the rough side of the cliff, moving so slowly they could hear their own steps.

Nathan looked back at Leslie. She was refusing to look any further than him and her feet. Her eyes were glazed.

Tiny stones and dirt slid from under their steps. Most of the face of the cliff was sandstone, crumbling at the touch. Nathan was using his knife to cut away obstacles as he went, but there wasn't much he could do about the ledge that held them from plunging to the land below.

They all prayed as they went sideways, flat against the cliff. As they neared the bottom, they were all out of breath. The last twenty feet, there was nothing but a steep drop. They began to slide down it.

Crashing like falling rock to the valley floor, they rolled into heaps. Leslie fell against Nathan, and he sat up, helping her to rest against him.

Timothy got to his feet and hurried over to them.

"Pa, you all right? Leslie?"

They looked around. Beeler was growling he broke the heel

151

off his boot. Chavez had cushioned Lupe's fall, and she was fussing over him. Quincy had hurt his pride.

But all of them were alive.

Suddenly, Timothy pointed up the cliff. "Pa, look."

They all stood up and stared.

Nathan's black mountain horse was coming down the cliff ledge a step at a time, head down, tail switching.

They were so amazed, they could not speak.

The horse worked its way slowly, carefully.

When it reached the last twenty feet of slide, it just sat on its rear and slid. When it hit the bottom, it sprang to its feet, unhurt. Nathan ran to it, catching the bridle.

"Old friend, you made it!"

The horse nuzzled him, and the others felt joy and relief. This country couldn't beat them after all.

"Hey," Beeler said to Nathan, "do I get my gold watch?"

"You earned it," Nathan said.

They moved out hurriedly, the women riding and the men walking, but they never saw the Apaches after that. And when they entered the small prairie town of Sage Brush Flats, it was first light. A few men were on the boardwalk, staring at them.

Later, after hot baths and some sleep at the hotel, they converged on the small cantina and ate their fill. Each was saying silent prayers of thanks.

Out on the boardwalk in the starlight, Nathan leaned on the railing. His son was at his side. Nathan had never felt so old and tired in his life. He wanted to start all over, to try to be young again. He had wasted too much time on the move. All of his travels now merged into a terrible feeling of emptiness. He was at the end of his trail.

"What now, Pa? You goin' away again?"

"Maybe, but you'd go with me."

"What about Leslie?"

He shrugged. "She's a fine lady. She can do better than what we'd have to offer, Timothy."

"Pa, ain't I big enough to be called Tim?"

Nathan grinned. "You bet you are."

"But what about Leslie?"

"She'd never even consider the likes of me."

"Don't you dare speak for me, Nathan Reed."

They turned as Leslie came to join them. She had washed her hair and it was silken in the pale light of the stars. She looked lovely. Nathan was suddenly very nervous.

He shrugged, straightening, backing away.

She followed, a smile on her face. "You're not getting away so easily."

He was speechless, staring at her boldness.

"Yeah, Pa, how about it? You and me and Leslie?"

Nathan felt cornered. "Well, I ain't sure I—"

"What are you afraid of, Nathan?" she asked.

He stood like stone. His grief had barely come under control, and now a beautiful woman was proposing. His heart lost its beat. He couldn't move. Instead, he just stood with his mouth open.

She gazed at him a long brave moment, her love for him shining in her eyes, and then she lost her courage. Tearfully, she turned away, walking down the boardwalk, away from them, not knowing where she was going.

"Pa, don't let her get away."

Nathan was cold and numb all over. He felt his son push him

away from the railing and toward Leslie. Now he was moving on his own, a little faster in the moonlight.

Leslie heard him coming and slowed her walk.

"Leslie," he said awkwardly, "I'm not going back to General Crook. These last few weeks, they near killed me. Maybe I'm gettin' old. But I want to laugh again, go fishing with my son, ride my own spread and throw rocks in the creek, rustle up wood for the fire, and stand on the porch with you and watch the sunset. So I'm askin'. Will you marry us?"

Her back to him, she was quiet a moment, and then she slowly turned to gaze at him. "You must promise, if you ever leave, no matter where you go, we go with you."

"I promise."

"But why me, Nathan?"

His face was burning. It was pure agony to drag out the truth on his parched lips. "Because I love you."

"Then it's yes, Nathan."

Nathan grinned. "Wowie."

Timothy ran over to them. "Yeah, wowie, Pa."

Nathan caught her up in his embrace, crushing her against him. She felt wonderful. He looked down into her wide blue eyes, his heart dancing as he bent his head and kissed her. She sure tasted good. She hugged him as they brought Timothy into the fold.

And in Leslie's arms with his son at his side, Nathan Reed gave a silent prayer of thanks.

ABOUT THE AUTHOR

Western novelist and screenwriter **Lee Martin** grew up on cattle ranches in Northern California. Martin began writing in the third grade and, later in life, wrote and sold 43 short stories before turning to novels with 23 now published. Martin is also a prolific writer of screenplays, mostly Westerns.

Martin's screenplay for *Shadow on the Mesa*, starring Kevin Sorbo, Wes Brown, and Gail O'Grady, was based on Martin's novel of the same title (Five Star Publishing, 2014). The movie was the second-highest-rated and second-most-watched original movie in Hallmark Movie Channel's history when it premiered in 2013. The film also won the prestigious Wrangler Award given by the National Cowboy & Heritage Museum in Oklahoma City for Best Original TV Western Movie.

Martin's recent novels, *The Grant Conspiracy*, *The Last Wild Ride*, and *Fury at Cross Creek*, all received rave reviews from *True West Magazine* and were based on Martin's screenplays, as is *Fast Ride to Boot Hill*. *In Mysterious Ways*, Martin's new modern suspense Western, received great critical acclaim from *Kirkus Reviews* and *Midwest Book Reviews*. *Trail of the Fast Gun* is the first book of seven in The Darringer Brothers series, all of which are reissued in paperback and ebook by Vaca Mountain Press.

Martin left the practice of law to write full-time, primarily concentrating on Western screenplays and novels, and often converting one to the other. Several of Martin's screenplays are currently under option by producers. To learn more, visit Lee Martin Westerns on Facebook.